The Wings of Aetheria: A Forbidden Journey of Magic and Freedom

Bound by fate, two lovers must rise above fear and embrace the magic that could unite or destroy their world.

Julianna Cubbage

Copyright © 2024 Julianna Cubbage

All rights reserved

The characters and events portrayed in this book are fictitious. Any similarity to real persons, living or dead, is coincidental and not intended by the author.

No part of this book may be reproduced, or stored in a retrieval system, or transmitted in any form or by any means, electronic, mechanical, photocopying, recording, or otherwise, without express written permission of the publisher.

Chapter 1: Cedric's Ordinary Life

Cedric Emerald was not, at first glance, anyone particularly remarkable. He was the son of a blacksmith and a seamstress in the small village of Oakmere, a place so nestled in the heart of Aetheria's greenest hills that the kingdom's grander towns might have been myth to anyone who lived there. Oakmere was a place of predictability, of days that flowed from one to the next like the gentle streams cutting through the village. It was beautiful, and it was safe. But Cedric often thought it was a world far too small for dreams.

At twenty years old, Cedric was known for his intense curiosity and for the spark in his striking emerald-green eyes. Those eyes were like gemstones that seemed to capture the flickering sunlight or glint with the same mischief that had gotten him into countless scrapes. More than once, he'd been found trying to scale the old watchtower on the village's northern edge or vanishing into the wild woods to see what lay beyond the trees.

But life in Oakmere rarely held the kind of adventure Cedric longed for. Villagers were content with their simple routines, with bread baking, crops growing, and festival days on the first full moon of each season. And if there were secrets to discover, no one seemed much interested in uncovering them. Magic, especially, was almost unheard of; it had once flowed through Aetheria, so legend said, but that had been before King Thaddeus Aether's rule. Cedric had heard whisperings of how the king feared magic, believing it a force of chaos and rebellion, and so he had driven it out of the kingdom.

Yet for Cedric, the very idea of magic was captivating. While he helped his father in the forge, shaping tools and horseshoes, he'd dream of what it would be like to wield a power all his own. When he explored the woods or lay beneath the open sky, he'd close his eyes and feel the wind rushing around him, almost as though he could rise up and soar with it. But every time he opened his eyes, the sky was only ever out of reach, an endless expanse that made him feel small.

One early autumn morning, Cedric found himself back in those woods, wandering down paths made familiar by his countless ventures. Sunlight filtered down through golden leaves, and the forest buzzed with life. As always, Cedric hoped for something unusual—a hint, a glimpse of something beyond the ordinary. But Oakmere's woods were stubbornly uneventful, yielding nothing more than the chatter of squirrels and the occasional startled deer.

He sighed, stopping to brush a few leaves off a large stone and sitting down. Looking around, he couldn't shake the feeling that he was meant to be somewhere else. But where? Adventure was a thing of stories, of wild tales spun by old men who could hardly tell you where truth ended and fiction began. Still, he couldn't help feeling that if he just kept searching, he'd find something.

And then, as if by fate, his eye caught a narrow trail winding off to the right, half-hidden by a tangle of roots and branches. He was sure he hadn't noticed it before, though he'd walked these woods a hundred times over. Cedric's curiosity flared, and without hesitation, he rose, ducked under the branches, and started down the path.

The trail wound deeper into the woods than any he'd ever followed. His heart beat faster with each step, the quiet thrill of the unknown tugging him forward. The air grew cooler, and the trees thickened until they blocked out much of the sunlight. After a while, Cedric began to wonder if he was wandering in circles. But before doubt could fully settle, he saw it—an ancient, crumbling tower just ahead, barely visible between two towering oaks.

The sight stopped him in his tracks. How could such a structure have been hidden all this time? Cedric felt a shiver of excitement. This was no ordinary ruin; something about it seemed... alive. Like it was waiting.

He approached slowly, his footsteps crunching on the brittle autumn leaves. The tower was covered in ivy, its stones cracked and weathered, but its door stood intact, an imposing piece of oak that looked far too sturdy for something so old. A strange energy hummed in the air around him, an odd sensation he could almost feel thrumming under his skin.

After a moment's hesitation, he pushed on the door. It creaked open, revealing a dark, dusty interior. Sunlight slanted through small, broken windows, casting dim light on what appeared to be a circular chamber. Empty shelves lined the walls, and in the center of the room stood a stone pedestal with a single object on top—a book, thick and bound in deep green leather, covered in dust as though it hadn't been touched for centuries.

Cedric approached the pedestal, feeling a pull that he couldn't explain. His hand hovered over the book, and he hesitated. Part of him, the cautious part, wanted to turn back and leave this place behind. But the rest of him—the restless, adventurous part—wanted nothing more than to see what lay within those pages.

As he reached out and touched the book's cover, a soft glow seemed to emanate from it, illuminating the symbols embossed on its surface. They were strange, curling shapes he didn't recognize, symbols that looked almost like spirals of wind and air. He brushed a layer of dust off the cover and, as he did, felt a jolt run through his hand.

The room seemed to darken around him, and for a moment, the world outside disappeared entirely. He felt a rush of energy, of something ancient and powerful stirring awake after a long slumber. The symbols on the book's cover began to shift and swirl, moving like clouds in a storm. Cedric's pulse raced, and he felt a warmth spreading from his fingertips up through his arm and into his chest.

It was as if the book was breathing, coming to life in his hands. Unable to resist, he opened it to the first page. Words appeared, shimmering faintly on the parchment. He couldn't understand their meaning, but he felt them, felt them deep within himself. Suddenly, a sharp breeze whipped through the tower, spiraling around him and lifting his hair. He closed his eyes as the wind swept around him, feeling lighter than he'd ever felt before.

When he opened his eyes, the book's light dimmed, and the wind died down. But something inside him had changed. He felt it—the power, the energy of the air, swirling within him. As he looked at his hands, he realized they tingled, like static coursing through his veins.

He could feel the wind now, not just as a passing force but as something alive, something he could call upon. His heart pounded with a mixture of awe and fear.

Had he just unlocked magic within himself?

Unsure what to make of this, Cedric closed the book, his mind racing. He glanced back toward the tower's door, knowing he couldn't stay here forever. But as he turned to leave, he caught sight of his reflection in a shard of cracked glass on the floor. His eyes, usually green as fresh leaves, now had a shimmer of silver, like a storm's edge.

Cedric left the tower that day as someone different. He'd come looking for adventure, but he'd found something else entirely. The world felt bigger now, and the air itself seemed to whisper secrets he'd never noticed before.

And he knew, deep down, that his life in Oakmere had just become too small to contain him.

Here's a full draft of Chapter 2: "The Fateful Discovery," where Cedric explores his newfound powers and the mystery of the ancient tome.

Chapter 2: The Fateful Discovery

The following days passed in a blur of cautious excitement. Cedric couldn't shake the feeling that something fundamental within him had shifted. He would catch himself staring at the sky, feeling an odd urge to reach out, like he could grasp the very air around him. The whisper of the wind carried a melody now, faint and elusive, calling him to try his newfound abilities again. But with a nervousness he couldn't entirely dispel, he'd return home to the forge each evening without attempting to call on the power he felt simmering within.

Eventually, his curiosity—and his need for answers—won out.

One crisp morning, Cedric packed a small satchel with bread and water and returned to the hidden tower, hidden beneath the forest's golden canopy. Inside, the dusty tome lay exactly as he had left it, resting on its pedestal. He could feel the book's presence calling to him, almost like a living thing. Taking a deep breath, he opened it once more, hoping to find guidance, anything that might explain what had happened to him.

The symbols on the pages seemed familiar now, yet still indecipherable. However, he noticed a faint change in them, a shimmer whenever he ran his fingers over the parchment. Cedric closed his eyes and focused, and without fully understanding how, he began to sense what each symbol meant. They weren't words so much as feelings—symbols that carried the essence of the wind, freedom, and motion.

Driven by instinct, he pressed his palm against one of the pages and whispered, "Show me."

The moment he spoke, the room filled with the sound of a rushing breeze, and he felt his body lighten, as though gravity itself had loosened its grip. Tentatively, he took a step forward, and to his amazement, his feet didn't touch the floor. He floated, weightless, hovering a few inches above the ground. A thrill shot through him, and he let out a laugh that echoed in the empty tower.

But his joy quickly shifted to alarm as he lost control, his body lurching upward. Desperately, he flailed his arms, trying to steady himself, but he only floated higher, bouncing lightly off the ceiling before finally managing to grab hold of a rafter. His heart pounded as he tried to calm himself, willing his feet back down to the floor. After a few tense moments, he lowered slowly, gently, until he was standing again, his legs shaking.

The rush of exhilaration lingered, and so did his uncertainty. He'd barely managed to keep himself from flying into the ceiling—how could he trust himself to do anything more? But as he looked back at the book, he felt a steadying reassurance, as though it were urging him to try again.

Over the next few days, he continued to return to the tower, experimenting in secret with the magic he had found within himself. Slowly, he grew more confident, discovering that he could control the wind to a surprising degree. He could conjure a breeze strong enough to lift leaves off the ground or gentle enough to barely ruffle his hair. And more than anything, he practiced the art of flight.

Each attempt brought him closer to control, to understanding how to make his movements intentional rather than wild or unpredictable. At first, he would only float a few inches off the ground, but each day he managed to lift himself higher, his confidence growing with every practice. The freedom he felt when he took to the air was exhilarating beyond anything he could have imagined. Flying felt like shedding the weight of the world, of everything that had ever kept him bound to Oakmere and its ordinary life.

But despite his growing skill, Cedric kept his power hidden from everyone in the village, not even daring to tell his parents. The thought of their reaction, and the inevitable rumors that would spread, held him back. Aetheria's people had long been taught to fear magic, to see it as something dangerous and forbidden. And while his powers filled him with wonder, Cedric could not forget that others might not share his sense of awe.

One evening, just as the sun dipped below the horizon, Cedric climbed to the top of a hill that overlooked Oakmere. The cool evening air wrapped around him, carrying the scents of woodsmoke and pine. He gazed down at the rooftops and winding streets of his village, feeling both a pang of longing and a rush of excitement. He wanted so badly to share this with someone—to tell them about the discovery that had changed his life.

As if answering his wish, a soft rustling behind him caught his attention. He turned to see a figure standing at the edge of the clearing—a young woman with long, golden hair that caught the last rays of sunlight, her sky-blue eyes sparkling with curiosity.

Cedric felt his breath catch. He had seen this girl before, though only from a distance. She was Ariana Skyward, the princess of Aetheria. She occasionally visited Oakmere, traveling with her royal retinue, and every villager knew of her beauty and her kindness. But seeing her here, alone, was something he never expected.

"Hello, Cedric," she said, her voice warm and soft, as though she were greeting an old friend. Her gaze held a depth that surprised him, as if she already knew more about him than he'd ever revealed to anyone.

"H-Hello, Princess Ariana," he stammered, suddenly aware of the dirt on his clothes and the tousled state of his hair. He gave a clumsy bow, but she laughed, a musical sound that put him at ease.

"No need for that," she replied. "I'm just Ariana."

Cedric nodded, still struggling to find his voice. "What brings you here… to Oakmere? And alone?"

Ariana's expression softened. "Sometimes, even a princess needs to be alone, away from… responsibilities," she said, choosing her words carefully. "And I have heard tales of Oakmere's peaceful woods. I wanted to see them for myself."

They stood in silence for a moment, gazing out over the hills as dusk settled around them. Finally, Ariana turned to him, her eyes filled with a knowing gleam.

"You can control the wind, can't you?" she asked, her voice barely above a whisper.

Cedric felt a shock course through him. He opened his mouth to deny it, to laugh it off as a joke, but something in Ariana's steady gaze told him she already knew the truth. She was not guessing.

"I… I don't know how you know that," he finally replied, "but yes. I discovered it recently, in the woods. It's something I've kept hidden."

Ariana nodded thoughtfully. "I sensed it," she said. "You see, I too have magic. I was born with it, though I've had to keep it hidden for as long as I can remember. It's… dangerous for someone like me to reveal it, but when I saw you, I knew we shared something special."

Cedric's heart pounded. To find someone else like him—a person who not only understood his abilities but shared them—was beyond anything he could have hoped for. "What kind of magic do you have?" he asked, his voice tinged with wonder.

"Air magic, just like you," she replied. "I can feel the wind, shape it, even ride it. It's something that's always been a part of me."

They spent the next hour sharing stories of their experiences, laughing as they recounted their first clumsy attempts to control the wind. Cedric felt an immediate connection with Ariana, a bond that seemed to transcend words.

She understood him in a way no one else could, and he found himself growing more at ease with every passing moment.

As the stars began to appear overhead, Ariana stood up, extending her hand to him. "Come with me," she said. "There's something I want to show you."

Without hesitation, Cedric took her hand, feeling a surge of warmth as their fingers intertwined. She led him to a clearing, where the open sky stretched above them in a vast expanse.

"Close your eyes and feel the wind," she whispered, releasing his hand.

Cedric did as she said, allowing himself to relax, to feel the currents of air swirling around him. With a deep breath, he opened his eyes—and saw Ariana rising into the air, her golden hair catching the starlight as she ascended. She glanced back at him, smiling, and held out her hand once more.

"Come on, Cedric. Let's soar together."

He took her hand, and together they rose, feeling the wind lift them higher and higher, carrying them into the night sky. In that moment, all his fears faded, replaced by the thrill of flight and the wonder of newfound companionship.

As they drifted over the treetops, laughing and weaving through the stars, Cedric knew that his life had changed forever. He was no longer alone, no longer bound to the earth. And beside him, Ariana's smile shone as brightly as the moon, a promise of the adventure yet to come.

Here's Chapter 3: "Hidden Bonds," where Cedric and Ariana begin to understand the depth of their shared connection and the risks of wielding magic in Aetheria.

Chapter 3: Hidden Bonds

The days that followed Cedric and Ariana's midnight flight passed like a dream. Cedric could hardly believe the life he'd led before—one limited to Oakmere, filled with the routine sounds of his father's forge, and framed by the same hillsides and the familiar faces of the village. Now, the world had cracked open to reveal endless possibilities. Every moment he spent with Ariana strengthened his conviction that he was destined for something beyond the narrow path he had always imagined.

They met in secret, under the cover of night or hidden in the forest's secluded clearings. Their practice sessions, which started with laughter and trial-and-error, quickly evolved into something deeper as Ariana taught Cedric the subtleties of air magic. She showed him how to shift a breeze with a flick of his fingers, how to create whirlwinds, and even how to silence his steps entirely by dampening the air around him.

"Magic isn't just about commanding the wind," she would remind him, her voice soft and serious. "It's about listening to it, feeling it as though it's part of you. If you try to force it, it will resist."

At first, Cedric found her words strange, but over time, he began to understand. There was a rhythm to the wind, a pulse that matched the beat of his own heart. Once he tapped into that harmony, he discovered he could coax the air into more complex shapes, crafting breezes that moved with purpose and subtlety. Ariana guided him patiently, her own expertise lighting the way.

But their bond grew far beyond their magical training. They shared stories of their lives—Cedric spoke of his family, his struggles with his father's expectations, and the sense of smallness he had always felt in Oakmere.

Ariana, in turn, spoke of the weight of her title, of being the princess expected to lead Aetheria someday. Her life, she confessed, had always felt like one long series of obligations. She was surrounded by advisors, servants, and nobles, but none of them truly saw her.

"With you," she said one evening, her gaze steady and searching, "I don't have to be the princess. I can just... be Ariana."

The words struck Cedric deeply. The sense of kinship between them was undeniable, as though they were two sides of the same coin. The more time he spent with her, the more he found himself drawn to her, not only because of their shared magic but because she understood him in a way no one else did. His feelings grew with every stolen moment, every shared glance, until he could hardly deny them any longer.

But as with all things precious, their bond carried a danger. They both knew it. Magic was not just forbidden—it was a threat to the balance of power in Aetheria. The fear of discovery lingered at the edges of their joy, a shadow that grew darker with every day that passed.

One evening, as the stars blinked into the sky, Ariana pulled Cedric aside, her face clouded with worry.

"Cedric," she whispered, her hand tight around his. "I fear that our meetings may not be as secret as we believe."

He looked at her, his heart pounding. "What do you mean?"

She hesitated, glancing over her shoulder before lowering her voice further. "My father... he has advisors who are, let's say, highly observant. One in particular, Lord Radomir, has long been suspicious of me. He's... ruthless. And ambitious. If he suspects that I have magic, he won't hesitate to use it against me. I fear he might already be watching us."

Cedric's blood ran cold. He had heard of Lord Radomir—rumors described him as a shrewd and calculating man with a fierce loyalty to the crown, but one who wielded that loyalty like a blade. A man who believed in his own vision for Aetheria's future, and who was willing to eliminate anything or anyone he saw as a threat.

"Why would he be watching you, though?" Cedric asked. "You've done nothing to betray your role as princess."

Ariana sighed. "Radomir knows how to exploit weakness. He's seen that I have no interest in wielding power the way he does. He's made comments, hints, as if he's waiting for me to slip up. If he had evidence of my magic… or worse, of us… he would use it to tighten his grip on the throne."

Cedric felt a wave of anger rise within him. The thought of anyone hurting Ariana, of exploiting her vulnerability for power, made his hands clench into fists. But she placed a hand on his arm, calming him.

"We have to be careful," she said, her voice firm. "Magic may feel like a gift, but in Aetheria, it is a curse—one that could bring ruin to both of us if we're not vigilant."

Their meetings became more cautious after that, always under the cover of night, always in the most secluded parts of the forest. Cedric found himself constantly glancing over his shoulder, searching the shadows for any sign of Radomir or his spies. The joy he had once felt in their shared magic was tinged with a sense of dread, as though each gathering could be their last.

But they could not stop. The bond between them had grown too strong, and Cedric could no longer imagine his life without her.

One night, as they practiced their magic beneath a sky thick with stars, Ariana turned to him, her expression solemn.

"I think it's time," she said quietly. "Time for us to find answers."

"Answers?" he echoed, puzzled. "What do you mean?"

She took his hand, her gaze intense. "There is someone who knows the ancient ways, someone who understands magic in a way few in Aetheria still do. A man named Eryndor, an old mage who lives in the mountains beyond the western forests. My mother once mentioned him when I was very young. She said he was a guardian of secrets, a keeper of knowledge from the time before magic was feared."

Cedric felt a thrill of excitement mixed with apprehension. "A mage... Are you certain he's real? And if he is, will he help us?"

Ariana nodded. "I believe he will. My mother trusted him once, and she rarely trusted anyone beyond her family. If anyone can help us understand what we are, and what we're meant to do, it's Eryndor."

The journey to find Eryndor would be long and perilous, but Cedric could feel the pull of destiny in her words. To meet a mage—a true wielder of ancient magic—would be to find the guidance they so desperately needed. And if they could learn more about their powers, perhaps they could discover a way to protect themselves from Radomir's suspicions.

But the journey was not without its risks. They would have to leave Oakmere and Aetheria's familiar landscapes behind, venturing into unknown territory, far beyond the safety of their hidden forest glades. Cedric thought of his parents, of the life he would leave behind, and felt a pang of guilt and fear.

Ariana sensed his hesitation and placed a comforting hand on his shoulder.

"I won't force you, Cedric," she said softly. "This choice must be yours. But I believe that if we stay here, hidden and afraid, we will only delay the inevitable. Radomir won't stop searching for something to use against me, and if we're not prepared, we may not survive his schemes."

Her words struck a chord within him. He knew that she was right—that hiding would not protect them forever. He thought back to the moment he had first felt the wind respond to his touch, the thrill and wonder that had ignited a fire within him. This magic was a part of him, of both of them, and it was calling them to something greater.

With a deep breath, he looked into her eyes and nodded. "I'm with you, Ariana. Whatever lies ahead, we'll face it together."

A smile lit up her face, and she squeezed his hand. "Then we leave at dawn."

They spent the rest of the night preparing for the journey, gathering supplies and planning their route through the forest. As the first light of dawn began to color the sky, they met at the edge of the woods, their cloaks pulled tightly around them.

Without a backward glance, they stepped onto the path that would lead them away from Oakmere, toward the mountains, and into the unknown.

Certainly! In Chapter 4, "Into the Unknown," Cedric and Ariana embark on their journey to find the mysterious mage Eryndor, discovering not only the challenges of the wilderness but also the secrets that lie within themselves.

Chapter 4: Into the Unknown

Cedric felt the morning chill seep into his bones as he and Ariana moved silently through the dense forest. Dawn's light barely penetrated the thick canopy of trees, casting long shadows over their path and adding an air of mystery to their journey. It felt strange to be leaving Oakmere behind, the only home he had ever known. But he pushed down any doubts and kept his gaze forward, determined to face whatever lay ahead with Ariana by his side.

They traveled in silence for a while, each step taking them further from the familiar and deeper into the unknown. Ariana's face was calm and composed, but he sensed the tension in her shoulders and the quiet urgency in her stride. They were both aware of the dangers they faced—not only from the wilderness but also from Lord Radomir's spies, who might have already noticed Ariana's absence.

"We should move quickly," Ariana whispered, glancing over her shoulder. "Once we're beyond the western forests, we'll be safer. Few of Radomir's men venture that far."

Cedric nodded. "Do you think he suspects anything yet?"

She paused, considering. "I don't know. Radomir is careful, always watching from the shadows. He might suspect something, or he might just sense that I'm… different." She cast him a thoughtful look. "But I'm willing to bet he doesn't yet realize just how much we know, or what we're capable of."

Her confidence bolstered Cedric's spirits, and he found himself hoping that maybe, just maybe, they could complete this journey unscathed. The thought of meeting Eryndor, of finding answers, gave him a renewed sense of purpose.

The day wore on as they traveled deeper into the forest, and the terrain grew more rugged. They crossed streams and wound through dense thickets, each step taking them further from Oakmere and closer to Eryndor's rumored home in the mountains. As they climbed higher, the air grew colder, and Cedric felt his fingers grow numb despite his cloak.

Ariana stopped suddenly, her gaze sharp. She gestured for Cedric to be silent, and they both froze, listening to the forest around them. In the stillness, he heard it too—a faint rustling, far too deliberate to be the wind or an animal. He held his breath, his senses alert.

"What is it?" he whispered.

Ariana's eyes narrowed as she scanned the trees. "We're not alone."

Cedric's heart pounded. Had Radomir's men somehow tracked them? He looked around, but the forest was dense, offering countless places for someone to hide. Slowly, Ariana raised her hand, her fingers flickering with a faint hint of magic. Cedric watched in awe as she extended her senses, the air around them bending slightly as she sent a small current of wind outward.

Moments later, a shadow moved in the trees—a figure cloaked in dark gray, stepping forward with a cautious yet steady gait. Cedric tensed, ready to defend them, but Ariana held up a hand.

The figure stopped a few paces away, lowering his hood to reveal a face lined with age but sharp with awareness. His piercing green eyes swept over them, and a faint smile tugged at the corners of his mouth.

"You're a hard pair to track down," he said, his voice surprisingly warm. "But I sensed you two had left Oakmere, and I felt… compelled to meet you."

Ariana tilted her head, studying the stranger. "Who are you?"

The man inclined his head. "My name is Theron. I'm… let's just say I have a vested interest in young mages like yourselves."

Cedric exchanged a quick glance with Ariana, his pulse quickening. "Are you… like us?" he asked, barely daring to hope.

Theron's smile widened, and he extended a hand, palm up. A faint glow appeared above his hand, swirling into a small, golden orb of light that hovered for a moment before fading. Cedric's breath caught. He had never seen magic used so effortlessly, so naturally.

"You could say that," Theron replied, lowering his hand. "Magic is a part of me, as it is of you both. And that's why I came. I sensed the awakening of your power and knew you would need guidance." His gaze softened as he looked at them. "Especially if you're seeking Eryndor."

Ariana stepped forward, her expression guarded but curious. "You know Eryndor?"

Theron nodded. "I do. Eryndor is… a guardian of sorts. An old friend who has dedicated his life to protecting the ancient knowledge of magic. But he doesn't take kindly to uninvited guests."

Cedric felt a flicker of doubt. "Then why are we seeking him? If he doesn't want to be found…"

"Because he will understand your purpose once he meets you," Theron interrupted, his voice firm. "Eryndor is cautious, yes. But he's also wise enough to recognize those who might carry on the legacy of magic. And from what I've sensed… you two are meant for something far greater than hiding your powers in secret."

Ariana's eyes sparkled with determination. "Then we'll do whatever it takes to gain his trust."

Theron studied them both for a long moment, his expression unreadable. Finally, he nodded. "Then allow me to guide you. The path to Eryndor's dwelling is treacherous, and it takes more than strength to reach him. You'll need skill, patience, and a clear purpose."

He gestured for them to follow, and Cedric felt a mixture of excitement and apprehension. Having a guide, someone who understood magic and knew Eryndor, felt like a stroke of luck. But he couldn't shake the feeling that their journey had just grown even more complicated.

They walked in silence for a while, Theron leading them through narrow paths and hidden trails that Cedric never would have noticed on his own. The forest grew darker as they ascended, the trees thickening until they blocked out most of the sunlight. Cedric stumbled on the rough ground, but Ariana caught his arm, steadying him. He glanced at her, grateful, and she offered him a small smile.

Theron finally stopped at the edge of a cliff overlooking a vast, misty valley. He turned to face them, his expression grave.

"Before we go further, you must understand the risks," he said. "Eryndor has guarded these secrets for centuries, and he will not share them lightly. He may test you, challenge you, perhaps even turn you away if he deems you unworthy. Are you prepared for that?"

Ariana didn't hesitate. "Yes. We came here for answers, and we won't turn back now."

Cedric nodded, though a knot of nervousness twisted in his stomach. He had never been tested in his life, never truly pushed to his limits. But he had Ariana by his side, and that gave him strength he never knew he had.

Theron's gaze softened slightly. "Very well. Remember, you're not just seeking knowledge. You're seeking understanding. Eryndor will expect you to prove yourselves not only in magic but in purpose."

With those cryptic words, Theron turned and led them down a narrow, winding path along the edge of the cliff. The wind whipped at them, cold and biting, and Cedric found himself drawing on the magic Ariana had taught him, using it to shield himself from the chill. Ariana did the same, her steps steady and sure despite the steep descent.

At the bottom of the path, Theron paused before a large stone archway half-hidden by ivy and moss. He placed a hand on the stone, murmuring a word that Cedric couldn't quite make out, and the air shimmered before them. A soft glow appeared, illuminating the entrance.

"This is where I leave you," Theron said, his voice tinged with a hint of sadness. "Eryndor's realm is beyond this point, and only those he calls may enter."

Cedric and Ariana exchanged a glance. They both felt it—the weight of the journey, the unknown challenges that lay ahead. But they had come this far, and there was no turning back.

"Thank you, Theron," Ariana said, her voice filled with gratitude. "We wouldn't have made it this far without you."

Theron inclined his head. "I believe in you both. Remember, magic is more than a tool. It's a bond—a force that connects all things. Trust in that bond, and you may find what you seek."

With those parting words, Theron stepped back, watching as Cedric and Ariana crossed the threshold into Eryndor's realm. The light faded behind them, and they found themselves in a vast, mist-shrouded landscape, filled with strange trees and ancient stones that seemed to pulse with energy.

Cedric felt a strange thrill, as though they were stepping into a world beyond time and space. Beside him, Ariana's face was set with determination, her eyes bright with anticipation.

Their journey had led them here, to the heart of ancient magic. And whatever awaited them, they were ready to face it together.

Chapter 5: The Trials Begin

As Cedric and Ariana stepped further into Eryndor's realm, a profound silence enveloped them. The mist thickened, muffling their footsteps and casting an eerie glow over the landscape. The ancient trees that surrounded them felt alive, their gnarled branches twisting in silent, watching forms.

Cedric's heart pounded. He sensed that every step forward brought them closer to something monumental, something that would test their courage in ways they couldn't yet imagine. Beside him, Ariana's face was tense but resolute, her eyes scanning the path ahead as if steeling herself for whatever was to come.

They walked for what felt like hours, time slipping away in the timelessness of this strange place. Eventually, they reached a clearing where a tall, stone structure loomed before them, partially covered in vines and etched with mysterious symbols. At its base was a pair of massive doors, carved with intricate patterns of stars and swirling winds. Cedric's breath caught; it was beautiful yet daunting, a testament to ancient powers beyond his understanding.

"This must be it," Ariana whispered, awe filling her voice. "The gateway to Eryndor's domain."

As they approached, the ground beneath them began to tremble softly. A faint hum filled the air, growing louder until it reverberated through Cedric's bones. The doors creaked open slowly, revealing a dark hallway lit by faint, flickering orbs of light.

"Are you ready?" Ariana asked, her voice steady but her eyes betraying a flicker of uncertainty.

Cedric nodded, swallowing his nerves. "Together."

They stepped through the doorway, and the moment they crossed the threshold, the heavy doors slammed shut behind them with a resounding thud. Cedric flinched, but Ariana took his hand, grounding him. She gave him a reassuring squeeze, and he felt his courage swell again.

The hallway led them deeper into the stone structure, each step taking them further from the outside world and into a place that felt detached from reality itself. Eventually, they reached a vast chamber where the air seemed to shimmer with power. The walls were lined with ancient scripts, written in a language neither of them could decipher.

As they moved further in, a soft voice echoed through the chamber, filling every corner with a resonant power.

"Who enters my domain?"

Cedric and Ariana froze, scanning the chamber for the source of the voice. There was no one else there, but the voice filled the space, as though the walls themselves were speaking.

"We seek knowledge," Ariana called out, her voice clear and unwavering. "We seek the guidance of Eryndor."

Silence fell, and then a figure began to materialize in the center of the room, emerging from thin air as though he had always been there, hidden from sight. A tall man with silver hair and piercing blue eyes stood before them, his robes flowing around him like wisps of smoke. His face was lined with age, yet his gaze held a fierce, almost otherworldly intelligence.

"I am Eryndor," he said, his gaze piercing them both. "And what makes you think you are worthy of my guidance?"

Cedric felt his mouth go dry. He had no answer prepared; he hadn't thought this far ahead. But before he could speak, Ariana stepped forward.

"We have journeyed far to find you," she said, her voice steady. "We seek to understand the magic that flows within us. And we wish to use it not for power, but for purpose. To protect our land from those who would abuse it."

Eryndor's eyes narrowed. "Noble words," he said slowly. "But words alone mean nothing here. If you truly seek knowledge, you must earn it." He raised his hand, and the air around them shifted, thickening as though a powerful force had just descended upon the room.

"You will face three trials," Eryndor continued, his voice echoing through the chamber. "Each will test a different part of you—your strength, your spirit, and your understanding of magic. Only if you succeed in all three will I consider granting you the knowledge you seek."

Cedric's heart raced. Trials? He felt woefully unprepared. But one look at Ariana's determined expression was enough to keep him from backing down. He squared his shoulders and met Eryndor's gaze.

"We accept," he said, his voice more confident than he felt.

Eryndor nodded. "Very well. Your first trial begins now."

The ground beneath them trembled, and the walls of the chamber shifted, dissolving and reforming into a dense forest. Cedric blinked in astonishment. They were no longer in the stone chamber but in the heart of a shadowy woodland, with towering trees stretching into a darkened sky.

Eryndor's voice echoed through the forest, disembodied yet as clear as if he were standing beside them. "Your first trial is a test of strength. Before you lies a creature born of magic, a guardian of this realm. You must overcome it without losing yourselves to fear or rage."

Cedric barely had a chance to process Eryndor's words before a deep, guttural growl filled the air. His blood ran cold as a massive creature emerged from the shadows—a beast that resembled a wolf, but larger and more menacing, with eyes that glowed a sickly green and fur bristling with dark energy. Its claws dug into the earth, leaving smoldering marks in the soil, and it let out a fierce, bone-chilling howl that echoed through the trees.

Ariana took a step back, her hand clutching the small dagger she kept at her side. "Cedric," she whispered, her voice tense. "We need to stay calm. Remember what Eryndor said."

Cedric nodded, swallowing hard. He focused on steadying his breathing, willing his fear into submission. He could feel the magic within him stirring, responding to his rising adrenaline. But he knew he had to control it, to use it wisely.

The creature lunged at them, its fangs bared and claws extended. Cedric reacted instinctively, raising his hands and channeling his magic outward. A shield of energy formed between them and the beast, deflecting its attack. The creature stumbled back, snarling in frustration.

Ariana didn't waste a moment. She extended her hand, sending a burst of fire toward the creature. The flames licked at its fur, causing it to shriek and back away. But it was resilient, and the fire only seemed to anger it more. With a furious growl, it lunged again, this time targeting Ariana.

Cedric's heart pounded as he watched her sidestep the creature's attack, her movements fluid and precise. He could see the strain in her expression, the concentration required to keep her magic in check. She wasn't just fighting the creature—she was fighting to stay in control of her own power, to prevent herself from being overwhelmed.

"We need to work together," she called out to him, her voice strained. "Use your magic to trap it. I'll try to weaken it from here."

Cedric nodded, focusing his energy. He raised his hands, directing his magic toward the ground beneath the creature. The earth responded to his command, shifting and forming a barrier of stone around the beast, trapping its legs in place. The creature snarled, struggling against the restraints, but Cedric held his focus, pouring his strength into maintaining the spell.

Ariana took a deep breath, extending her hand once more. A bright, searing light appeared in her palm, growing brighter with each passing moment. Cedric watched in awe as she released the light, sending it straight toward the creature. The light enveloped the beast, and it let out a final, anguished roar before collapsing to the ground, defeated.

Silence fell over the forest as the creature faded into mist, its form dissolving until there was nothing left but the faint scent of charred earth. Cedric and Ariana stood side by side, breathing heavily, their hearts pounding from the intensity of the battle.

"Well done," Eryndor's voice echoed through the trees, carrying a hint of approval. "You have passed the first trial. You demonstrated strength not only in magic but in restraint—a rare quality for those so young."

The forest around them began to fade, dissolving back into the stone chamber. Cedric felt the solid ground beneath him once more, and he realized just how much energy the battle had taken. His muscles ached, and he could feel the toll that using his magic had taken on his body.

But there was no time to rest. Eryndor's gaze was sharp, and his voice held a warning. "The second trial will test your spirit, your resolve. Prepare yourselves."

Before Cedric could catch his breath, the room shifted again, and he and Ariana were plunged into darkness.

Chapter 6: The Test of Spirit

Cedric blinked, adjusting his eyes to the darkness that enveloped him. The chamber they'd been in was gone, replaced by an all-consuming void. He reached out instinctively, hoping to find Ariana, but his hand grasped nothing. Panic bubbled within him. Was he alone?

"Ariana?" he called out, his voice echoing through the emptiness.

"I'm here!" Her voice came, faint yet reassuring, as if she were far off. "I... I can't see you. Are you alright?"

Relief washed over him at the sound of her voice, but the darkness felt oppressive, thick with a strange energy. Cedric could feel it tugging at his heart, pulling memories and emotions he thought he'd buried. The feeling was unlike anything he'd experienced before, as though the darkness wasn't just around him—it was inside him.

Eryndor's voice echoed through the void, cold and distant. "This is the second trial, the Test of Spirit. Here, you will face your deepest fears, your doubts, and the shadows that reside within your heart. Only by confronting them will you pass."

A chill ran down Cedric's spine. His deepest fears? He'd faced dangerous creatures, magic-wielding foes, and the unknown depths of the forest. But this—this was different. This trial wasn't about his physical strength or magical abilities; it was about something deeper, more personal. The thought made his chest tighten.

"Ariana?" he called again, but this time, there was no response. He was truly alone now.

Suddenly, the darkness shifted, forming shapes and flickers of light. The air grew colder, and Cedric found himself standing on the edge of a cliff, overlooking a dark, churning sea. The sky was a turbulent mass of storm clouds, lightning flashing and illuminating the waters below. Cedric's heart pounded as he took a step back. The scene felt hauntingly familiar, and he realized with a sinking feeling that he'd been here before—in a memory he'd tried to forget.

It was the night he'd lost his older brother, Lysander.

Years ago, they'd been adventuring near the cliffs of their village, as they often did, daring each other to go closer to the edge. But that day, the wind had been fierce, and a sudden gust had caught Lysander off guard. Cedric had reached out to grab him, but his hand had slipped, and Lysander had fallen into the raging sea below. Cedric could still remember the helplessness, the feeling of being powerless as he watched his brother disappear into the waves.

Guilt clawed at him, raw and unrelenting. He'd carried this burden for so long, never forgiving himself for what had happened. And now, as he stood on the edge of the same cliff, the memory felt as real as the day it had happened. A voice whispered in his ear, soft and haunting.

"It was your fault, Cedric."

He spun around, but no one was there. The voice continued, relentless.

"If you'd been stronger, faster, braver... you could have saved him."

Cedric's throat tightened. He wanted to protest, to shout that he'd done everything he could. But deep down, he'd always feared that the voice was right—that he was responsible for Lysander's death. It was a weight he'd carried alone, never sharing it with anyone.

"No," he murmured, his voice shaking. "I... I couldn't have saved him. It was an accident."

But the voice persisted, growing louder. "You failed him, Cedric. Just like you'll fail everyone else who depends on you. You're weak, afraid, and unworthy of the power you seek."

The words struck like a blow to his chest. He sank to his knees, feeling the full weight of his guilt pressing down on him. How could he protect others if he couldn't even protect his own family? The darkness around him seemed to close in, wrapping him in despair.

Just when he thought he might drown in it, he heard another voice—faint but steady. A voice filled with warmth and hope.

"Cedric."

It was Ariana's voice, clear and grounding. He looked up, his vision blurred by tears, and saw a faint, glowing figure in the distance. She was reaching out to him, her hand extended, her face filled with compassion.

"Cedric, you have to forgive yourself," she said gently. "Lysander's loss wasn't your fault. You did everything you could. Sometimes, things happen that we can't control, no matter how hard we try."

He took a shaky breath, his mind fighting the voice of guilt that still whispered in his ear. But as he looked at Ariana, something inside him began to shift. He realized that he'd never truly allowed himself to grieve, never let himself confront the pain he'd buried so deeply.

Closing his eyes, he whispered, "I'm sorry, Lysander. I'm sorry I couldn't save you." The words felt like a release, as though he were finally letting go of a weight he'd carried for far too long. The guilt didn't vanish completely, but it lessened, replaced by a bittersweet ache that felt more bearable.

When he opened his eyes again, the cliff and the stormy sea had disappeared. The darkness receded, and he found himself standing back in the stone chamber, Ariana at his side, her hand resting on his shoulder.

"You did it," she said softly, her eyes filled with pride. "You faced it."

Cedric managed a small, grateful smile. "Thank you, Ariana. I... I don't think I could have done it without you."

She shook her head. "You had the strength within you all along, Cedric. Sometimes, we just need someone to remind us of it."

Before he could respond, Eryndor's voice echoed through the chamber once more. "Impressive, Cedric. You have faced your inner darkness and emerged stronger. But remember, the shadows within us are always there. True strength is acknowledging them, not being controlled by them."

Cedric nodded, taking Eryndor's words to heart. He felt different—lighter, somehow. Facing his guilt had been terrifying, but he understood now that it was a part of him, something he could accept rather than suppress.

Ariana squeezed his shoulder. "Are you ready for the final trial?"

He took a deep breath, feeling a newfound sense of clarity and resolve. "Yes. Whatever it is, we'll face it together."

Eryndor appeared before them, his gaze piercing and solemn. "The third trial is a test of understanding. Magic is not merely a tool or a weapon; it is an energy that flows through all things, a balance between creation and destruction. To wield it wisely, you must understand its nature."

He raised his hand, and the chamber around them transformed once again. They found themselves standing in a lush, verdant forest, with streams of sunlight filtering through the canopy. The air was filled with the sound of birdsong and the gentle rustle of leaves.

"In this final trial," Eryndor said, his voice softer, "you must prove that you understand the true essence of magic. Only then will I grant you the knowledge you seek."

Cedric looked around, unsure of what they were meant to do. The forest was peaceful, serene—a stark contrast to the challenges they'd faced so far. Ariana stood beside him, her brow furrowed in thought.

"What do you think he means by 'understanding'?" she asked.

Cedric considered this. He'd always thought of magic as something to be controlled, directed. But the way Eryndor spoke of it suggested something deeper, a connection that went beyond spells and incantations.

He closed his eyes, reaching out with his senses. He felt the warmth of the sunlight, the coolness of the breeze, the gentle hum of life all around him. Magic wasn't just an external force; it was a part of everything, a delicate balance that existed within him, within Ariana, within the forest itself.

"We need to be still," he murmured, opening his eyes and looking at Ariana. "We need to listen."

She nodded, understanding dawning in her expression. Together, they sat on the forest floor, closing their eyes and allowing themselves to become attuned to the world around them. They listened to the rhythm of the forest, the pulse of life that flowed through every leaf, every stone, every creature.

Slowly, Cedric felt a warmth spread through him—a gentle, soothing energy that resonated with his own magic. It wasn't something he could control; it was something he could connect with, something he could harmonize with.

When he opened his eyes, Eryndor stood before them, a faint smile on his face.

"You have passed the final trial," he said, his voice filled with approval. "You have learned that magic is not just a power to wield but a force to respect, to understand. Those who seek mastery over magic without understanding its nature often bring about their own ruin."

Cedric and Ariana exchanged a glance, a sense of accomplishment and humility washing over them.

Eryndor extended his hands, and in his palms, two glowing orbs of light appeared. "As promised, I will share with you the knowledge you seek. Take this gift, and may you use it wisely."

Cedric reached out, feeling the warmth of the orb as it merged with his own energy. It was as if a door had opened within him, revealing depths of magic he hadn't known existed. He glanced at Ariana, who looked equally awed.

"Thank you, Eryndor," Cedric said, his voice filled with gratitude. "We will honor this gift."

E

ryndor nodded solemnly. "Remember, the journey of understanding is never truly over. But with each step, you grow closer to the wisdom that lies at the heart of all things."

With those words, Eryndor faded into the forest, leaving Cedric and Ariana alone once more. They stood in silence for a moment, each of them absorbing the weight of what they'd experienced.

Finally, Ariana broke the silence. "We did it."

Cedric smiled, feeling a profound sense of peace. "Yes, we did. And I think... I think we're ready for whatever comes next."

Chapter 7: A New Purpose

Cedric and Ariana returned to the small clearing where they had initially met Eryndor. It was quiet now, the air carrying the familiar sounds of the forest, birds singing above them and a gentle breeze stirring the leaves. They had passed all three trials and now felt a profound sense of connection with magic—a connection that was less about control and more about harmony.

Ariana looked at Cedric, her eyes bright with excitement and a hint of wonder. "I can't believe we made it through," she said, a smile spreading across her face. "After everything we faced, I feel… different. Lighter, somehow. Do you feel it too?"

Cedric nodded, struggling to find the right words. The darkness he had faced, his lingering guilt over Lysander's death, and his newfound understanding of magic had left him feeling more centered, as if he had peeled away layers he hadn't realized were there. "It's like I can finally breathe fully again," he replied, returning her smile. "I feel clearer, and… more certain of what I need to do."

She raised an eyebrow, curiosity glinting in her gaze. "And what's that?"

Cedric took a deep breath, gathering his thoughts. The trials had revealed not only the power of magic but the responsibility that came with it. He couldn't shake the memory of Eryndor's words about respecting magic, understanding it as part of the natural order. Suddenly, his purpose was as clear as day.

"I need to return to our village," he said firmly. "There are people there who could benefit from what I've learned. For so long, I thought I needed to be somewhere else, chasing after greatness or adventure to feel worthy. But maybe my real purpose is closer to home."

Ariana smiled, a look of understanding in her eyes. "I think you're right, Cedric. We came all this way, and yes, it was to gain magical knowledge. But the journey was about so much more than that. We faced our fears, found clarity, and realized what truly matters. I'd like to come with you."

The offer warmed him deeply. He hadn't thought to ask, assuming she'd return to her own home after their quest. But the thought of continuing this journey with her felt right, as though she were meant to be by his side.

"I'd be honored," he said, his voice full of gratitude. "Together, I think we could do a lot of good."

Just then, a subtle glow appeared in the clearing, and Eryndor re-emerged from the trees, his gaze thoughtful as he looked between the two of them.

"Cedric, Ariana," he began, his voice as calm as ever, though this time with a softer warmth. "You've proven yourselves worthy of the power you now possess. But remember, knowledge and power are only as good as what you do with them. Your trials were only the beginning. Many challenges await you, and your resolve will be tested. But if you keep the spirit you showed here, you will find strength beyond what any magic can give."

Cedric and Ariana exchanged a glance, both humbled and inspired by his words.

"What should we do next?" Ariana asked, her voice steady but respectful.

"Follow your instincts," Eryndor replied. "There are people who need you. Use what you've learned to guide and protect them. Magic is a tool, yes, but it is also a bridge—one that connects those who wield it to the lives and hearts of others. Seek to understand, to connect, to help, and you will find your true path."

Cedric bowed his head, feeling a surge of purpose coursing through him. "Thank you, Eryndor. For everything."

Eryndor gave a nod, then turned his gaze to Ariana. "You have a gift, Ariana. An understanding of magic that goes beyond most. I believe you will be a guiding force for many who are lost. Stay true to your spirit, and you will find the wisdom you seek."

Ariana blushed slightly but nodded, a determined look in her eyes. "I won't let you down."

Eryndor smiled. "Then go, both of you. The journey is yours now."

With that, he raised his hand, and the world around them shifted once more. The forest faded, replaced by the familiar surroundings of the path they'd taken to Eryndor's hidden sanctuary. They were back on the edge of the dense woodlands, where sunlight streamed through the trees, casting dappled shadows along the ground. It felt strange to be back, knowing how much had changed within them.

They stood there for a moment, adjusting to the sudden brightness, then began walking down the path that would eventually lead back to their village. Neither of them spoke for a while, each lost in thought, absorbing the magnitude of what they had experienced.

As they walked, Cedric noticed something different. He could sense the energy in the trees, feel the pulse of life in the ground beneath his feet. The forest no longer felt like a place of mystery or danger; it felt familiar, alive, and full of wonder. He looked over at Ariana, wondering if she felt the same, and she met his gaze with a knowing smile.

"You feel it, don't you?" she asked.

He nodded. "It's like I can hear the forest breathing."

She laughed softly, a sound that blended with the whispers of the wind. "It's always been there. We just didn't know how to listen before."

As they continued down the path, Cedric's mind returned to the village and the people he cared about. He thought of his mother, who had always believed in him, and his friends who had supported him despite his doubts. He realized how much he wanted to share this newfound wisdom with them, to help protect them in ways he hadn't been able to before.

They arrived at the outskirts of the village by dusk, the golden light of the setting sun casting a warm glow over the familiar cottages and winding paths. Cedric felt a surge of warmth as he took in the scene. For the first time in a long time, he felt at peace—like he had come home not only to his village but to himself.

They headed toward the town square, where a small crowd had gathered, their faces alight with curiosity and relief. Cedric's mother was among them, and when she saw him, her face broke into a smile that made his heart swell.

"Cedric!" she called, hurrying over to embrace him. "You're back! We were so worried."

He hugged her tightly, savoring the warmth and comfort of her presence. "I'm here, Mother. And I'm… different now. I have so much to tell you."

The villagers gathered around, eager to hear of his journey, but Cedric held up a hand, glancing over at Ariana, who stood by his side with an encouraging smile.

"We've learned a lot," Cedric began, addressing the crowd, "but the most important thing we discovered is that magic is more than power. It's a connection, a way to help and protect each other. And I promise you, Ariana and I will use what we've learned to keep our village safe."

There were murmurs of approval and gratitude, and he felt the weight of their trust settle on his shoulders—a weight he was now ready to bear.

As the villagers dispersed, Cedric and Ariana lingered in the square, watching the stars appear one by one in the evening sky.

"What do you think comes next?" Ariana asked, her voice soft.

Cedric looked up at the stars, a sense of calm filling him. "I'm not sure. But I think we'll find our way. Together, we'll protect what we love and help others see the beauty of magic, just like Eryndor taught us."

Ariana smiled, taking his hand in hers. "Then let's start by being the guardians our village needs. Who knows where the journey will lead?"

They stood there in companionable silence, their hearts filled with purpose and their spirits intertwined, ready to face whatever lay ahead. The journey wasn't over; in many ways, it was only beginning. But for the first time, Cedric felt that he had everything he needed—courage, wisdom, and a friend by his side.

And with that, he knew they would be ready for whatever the future held.

Chapter 8: Trials of Leadership

As the days turned into weeks, Cedric and Ariana settled into their new roles within the village. Word of their journey spread quickly, and the villagers sought them out with questions, curiosities, and, sometimes, pleas for help. For Cedric, the transition felt natural in some ways but jarring in others. He had always thought of himself as just another face in the crowd, yet now he was looked upon as a figure of guidance and wisdom.

Ariana handled her newfound responsibility with grace, her innate connection to magic evident in the way she interacted with the villagers. She would gather the children in the mornings, showing them small, harmless spells that demonstrated the beauty of magic—the way flowers bloomed at her touch or how a breeze seemed to dance at her call. She encouraged them to respect magic as a tool for peace and unity, never for harm.

Cedric, meanwhile, was often approached by the village's elders and those who had grown wary of change. His challenge was different. He had to learn to balance his desire to protect the village with the need to respect the fears and reservations of the people who had known a different way of life. Many were skeptical of the power he now possessed, fearing that magic would bring trouble to their quiet existence.

One evening, he found himself in conversation with Mara, one of the oldest villagers and someone who had always been cautious about magic.

"I worry, Cedric," she said, her eyes narrowing as she looked at him. "Magic is a force that none of us truly understand. Do you think you can control it? Do you think it will not lead us into danger?"

Cedric met her gaze with a calmness he hadn't known he possessed. "I don't pretend to control magic, Mara. If there's one thing I've learned, it's that magic is not meant to be controlled but respected. We're only here to ensure it serves the village and to protect our people with what we know."

She sighed, still unconvinced. "Protect us, you say. But what if others come? What if they seek out our village because of the power you now hold?"

Cedric had thought of this often. The knowledge he and Ariana possessed could indeed attract those who wished to misuse it, or those who feared it enough to try to destroy it. He knew his promise to protect wasn't just a guarantee against external threats but a commitment to the people who had known him long before his journey began.

"If others come, we'll be ready," he said, his voice firm. "But I want you to understand that our purpose isn't to wield magic as a weapon. Ariana and I learned that magic is a way to connect, to protect, and to heal. I don't want to lead us into conflict—I want to help us find peace with it."

Mara studied him carefully, and for a moment, he saw a flicker of understanding in her eyes. "Perhaps there's truth in your words, Cedric. But we'll be watching."

As she walked away, he felt the weight of his promise grow heavier, and he knew that the trust of the village would not come easily. He would need to earn it every day.

A few days later, a visitor arrived from a neighboring village, bringing word of a sickness spreading through the farms on the outskirts of their territory. It was unlike any illness the villagers had seen, and the healers were at a loss for how to contain it. Cedric and Ariana listened intently as the visitor, a young man named Rowan, described the symptoms—a strange fever that didn't respond to traditional remedies and left those afflicted weak and drained.

"It's spreading fast," Rowan said, his eyes filled with worry. "We've tried everything we know, but nothing works. They say you have magic now. Perhaps you can do something?"

Cedric glanced at Ariana, and she gave a slight nod, her eyes reflecting the same determination he felt. "We'll do everything we can to help," Cedric assured him.

The two packed supplies and left with Rowan the next morning, setting out on the path to the neighboring village. Along the way, they spoke with Rowan, asking for any details that might help them understand the illness. He described how the sickness had appeared suddenly, affecting the young and old alike, and how it left even the strongest villagers too weak to walk.

When they arrived, the sight was sobering. The village square was empty, and the few people they saw were hurried, with worried expressions and red-rimmed eyes. Rowan led them to a small building where the sick were gathered. Inside, the air was thick with the scent of herbs and damp cloths, and soft groans filled the room.

Ariana knelt beside one of the patients, a young girl with pale skin and a sheen of sweat on her forehead. She placed a hand on the girl's wrist, closing her eyes in concentration. Cedric watched as a faint glow emanated from Ariana's hand, a soft, reassuring light that seemed to calm the girl's fevered breathing.

"It's strange," Ariana murmured after a moment. "This isn't a natural illness. There's a trace of magic here, something dark."

Cedric's heart sank. If the illness was magical in nature, it meant someone had cast a spell—someone who intended harm.

"Is there anything we can do?" he asked, keeping his voice low so as not to alarm the villagers.

Ariana nodded, though her expression was grave. "I think I can isolate the magic and counteract it, but it will take time. And I'll need your help to keep it from spreading."

They spent the next several hours working together, casting spells to contain the dark energy that lingered within the afflicted villagers. It was exhausting work, requiring constant focus and precision. Ariana's face grew pale, beads of sweat forming on her brow, but she refused to rest until she had done all she could for each patient.

Cedric, meanwhile, worked to reinforce the spells, stabilizing the magic and ensuring it remained contained. The villagers watched in awe, their initial skepticism giving way to quiet gratitude. For the first time, Cedric felt as if they were truly making a difference, using their knowledge not just to defend but to heal.

By the time they finished, the sun had set, and the village was quiet. The patients rested peacefully, their breathing steady and calm. Cedric and Ariana sat outside, weary but filled with a deep sense of accomplishment.

"That was incredible," Cedric said, looking at Ariana with admiration. "You saved them."

She shook her head, a faint smile on her lips. "We saved them, Cedric. I couldn't have done it alone."

They sat in silence for a while, watching the stars. For Cedric, the experience had solidified his purpose, reminding him that magic was a tool for compassion as much as it was for protection. He thought of the doubts that had lingered in his mind, the fears that he would never be enough. But here, in this quiet village, he realized that he was exactly where he needed to be.

The following morning, they prepared to return home, bidding farewell to the villagers who had gathered to thank them. Rowan, the young man who had brought them here, approached Cedric and Ariana with a look of gratitude.

"You've given us hope," he said, his voice thick with emotion. "I don't know what we would have done without you."

Cedric placed a hand on his shoulder. "You're part of our community too. If you ever need help, you can count on us."

As they left the village, walking side by side along the winding path, Cedric felt a renewed sense of clarity. He was no longer the uncertain young man who had left his village seeking purpose. He had found it here, in the quiet moments of healing and in the bonds he had forged with those who needed him.

They returned to their village as dawn broke over the trees, casting a golden light on the familiar cottages and fields. Cedric knew that challenges would continue to arise—that doubt and fear might still creep into his mind. But he also knew that, with Ariana by his side and his commitment to his village guiding him, he would face whatever came next.

As they walked into the village square, greeted by smiles and nods from familiar faces, Cedric felt a warmth spread through him. He had found his place, his purpose. And though the journey was far from over, he was ready for whatever lay ahead.

Chapter 9: Whispers of Darkness

The weeks following their journey to the neighboring village passed quietly. Cedric and Ariana continued to fulfill their roles, each day strengthening their bond with the villagers and deepening their understanding of magic's role in their lives. Peace had settled over the village, and with it came a sense of purpose that both Cedric and Ariana had longed for.

But peace, they soon learned, was fragile.

One evening, as Cedric was walking through the village square, he noticed a man he didn't recognize lingering near the edge of the forest. Dressed in a dark cloak, the man moved with a quiet, purposeful grace, his eyes scanning the village as though he were searching for something—or someone. Cedric's instincts prickled with unease. He approached the stranger, keeping his expression neutral but his senses alert.

"Good evening," Cedric greeted him. "Can I help you with something?"

The man looked at Cedric, his gaze sharp and assessing. "I'm merely passing through," he replied in a low voice, his tone polite but guarded.

Cedric nodded, though he sensed there was more to the man's presence than he was letting on. "Are you a traveler?" he asked, trying to keep the conversation light.

"In a sense," the man replied, his lips curving into a faint smile. "I'm here to study… to observe the world and its changes. It's said that this village has experienced quite a few changes of its own recently."

Cedric's unease grew. He had been careful to keep his and Ariana's use of magic discreet, but word still spread quickly between villages. He was suddenly aware that their efforts to protect and heal had drawn attention, not just from allies but from those who might see their power as something to exploit—or extinguish.

"Change is natural," Cedric replied carefully, his voice calm. "We're simply doing our best to care for each other."

The man inclined his head, a glint of something unreadable in his eyes. "Indeed. Caring for one's own is commendable. But there are those who see magic as a force too dangerous to be left unchecked."

Cedric's heart pounded. The stranger's words were veiled, but the warning was clear. He chose his next words with care. "Magic can be a powerful tool when used wisely. It's only a danger if wielded recklessly."

The man's gaze sharpened, and for a brief moment, a flicker of something dark flashed in his eyes. "Wise words," he said softly. "But wisdom can only take one so far. Power, on the other hand, has a way of attracting those who seek control, regardless of their wisdom."

With that, the man turned and disappeared into the shadows of the forest, leaving Cedric standing alone in the square, his mind racing. He had encountered danger before, but this felt different. There was an intent behind the stranger's words, a subtle threat that hinted at forces far greater than Cedric had ever faced.

When Cedric told Ariana about the encounter later that night, she listened intently, her brow furrowed in thought. "Whoever he was, he clearly knows more than he's letting on," she said, a note of worry in her voice. "We should be cautious."

Cedric nodded. "I agree. We've been careful, but it seems that word of our magic is spreading faster than we realized. I don't want to alarm the village, but we need to prepare for the possibility that others might come, with intentions far worse than this man's."

Ariana placed a reassuring hand on his arm. "We're in this together, Cedric. Whatever comes, we'll face it as a team."

Her words steadied him, and he felt a renewed sense of determination. They had worked too hard to build a life here, to find purpose and connection. He wasn't about to let a shadowy stranger threaten what they had fought to create.

In the days that followed, Cedric and Ariana began fortifying the village in subtle ways, placing protective wards along the outskirts and strengthening the spells that concealed their presence from those who sought to do harm. They taught the villagers simple defensive charms, just enough to protect themselves without drawing attention. Cedric noticed that Mara, the elder who had once been wary of magic, was now one of their most diligent students, a quiet determination in her eyes as she practiced each spell with care.

Despite their precautions, Cedric couldn't shake the feeling that something darker was lurking, waiting for the right moment to strike. The stranger's warning echoed in his mind, a reminder that power, even when used for good, had a way of drawing attention. And not all attention was welcome.

One evening, as Cedric and Ariana sat by the fire, a sudden gust of wind rattled the windows, extinguishing the flames and plunging the room into darkness. They exchanged a tense glance, both sensing the shift in the air. It was more than just the wind—there was a presence, something foreign and menacing.

Ariana rose, her hand outstretched as she whispered a spell, reigniting the fire. But as the flames flickered to life, they cast a twisted shadow across the wall, revealing a figure cloaked in darkness standing just outside the window.

Cedric leaped to his feet, moving toward the door, but the figure vanished as quickly as it had appeared, leaving behind a faint trail of smoke and a lingering sense of dread.

"That wasn't just a stranger," Ariana murmured, her voice barely above a whisper. "That was magic—a dark, ancient magic."

Cedric's jaw tightened. He had encountered dark magic before, but this felt different, more insidious. It was as if the darkness itself was alive, seeking them out with an intelligence that went beyond mere malice.

"We need to find out who's behind this," he said, his voice steely with resolve. "If there's someone using dark magic to watch us, they won't stop until they get what they want."

Ariana nodded, her face pale but determined. "Agreed. But we can't do this alone. We need allies—others who understand the dangers of dark magic and can help us protect the village."

They spent the next few days reaching out to neighboring villages, seeking out anyone with knowledge of dark magic and its origins. They learned of a reclusive mage named Lysandra who lived deep within the forest, rumored to possess knowledge of ancient spells and the wisdom to counteract dark forces. It was said that she had once walked the line between light and dark magic, using her powers to protect those who could not protect themselves.

Determined, Cedric and Ariana set out at dawn, following a winding path through the dense forest. The journey was treacherous, the path overgrown and shrouded in mist, but they pressed on, guided by the faint traces of magic that lingered in the air.

After hours of walking, they reached a small clearing where a modest stone cottage stood, ivy crawling up its walls and the air thick with the scent of herbs and earth. As they approached, the door creaked open, and a figure stepped into the light.

Lysandra was an older woman, her face lined with age but her eyes sharp and clear. She regarded them with a mixture of curiosity and caution. "I know why you're here," she said, her voice low and commanding. "Darkness has found you, and it will not leave until it is satisfied."

Cedric and Ariana exchanged a glance, surprised by her directness. "Can you help us?" Cedric asked, his voice filled with both hope and urgency.

Lysandra studied them for a long moment, her gaze piercing. "I can teach you to protect yourselves," she said finally. "But know this—dark magic is not easily defeated. It feeds on fear, on doubt. If you are to face it, you must be prepared to confront the darkness within yourselves as well."

They both nodded, resolute. Cedric felt a surge of determination. He had come too far, faced too many trials, to back down now. Together, he and Ariana would face whatever darkness awaited them, armed with the strength of their bond and the knowledge they had gained.

Over the next several days, Lysandra taught them spells and rituals that had been forgotten by most, knowledge passed down through generations of mages who understood the delicate balance between light and dark. She showed them how to weave magic into the fabric of their surroundings, creating barriers that would confuse and repel those with ill intentions.

Through it all, she reminded them of one crucial truth: dark magic could not be defeated by force alone. It required understanding, patience, and, most importantly, an unbreakable will.

As they prepared to return to their village, Lysandra gave them one final piece of advice. "Remember," she said, her gaze solemn, "the darkness will test you. It will try to twist your mind, to turn you against each other. But as long as you trust in each other, as long as you remember who you are, it cannot defeat you."

With her words ringing in their ears, Cedric and Ariana made their way back home, their hearts steeled against the trials to come. The village awaited them, and so did the shadows—but this time, they were ready. They would face whatever darkness came their way, and they would do so together, bound by their shared purpose and an unyielding resolve.

Chapter 10: Shadows in the Light

The village lay quiet under the light of the waning moon as Cedric and Ariana returned from their journey. Their minds buzzed with everything they had learned from Lysandra, each spell and incantation feeling like an armor they had donned against the creeping darkness. But even with this newfound knowledge, the atmosphere felt heavier than before, as though the air itself held a warning.

The villagers, as if sensing an unseen threat, had taken on an air of wary vigilance. Children played closer to home, and even the animals seemed to avoid the forest's edge. Cedric and Ariana could feel the weight of it, a constant reminder that something, or someone, was watching.

In the days that followed, Cedric and Ariana began integrating Lysandra's teachings into their daily routines. They reinforced the protective wards surrounding the village, embedding spells into the very soil. Together, they crafted barriers to cloak the village in layers of enchantments, hoping to keep the shadows at bay.

But the darkness was cunning.

One night, as Cedric made his rounds to inspect the wards, he noticed a flicker at the edge of the barrier—a shadow, faint but unmistakable, pressing against the magic. It was a subtle intrusion, like a whisper pressing against glass, yet powerful enough to ripple through his wards. He moved closer, his instincts on high alert, and murmured a counter-spell, willing the barrier to hold.

Yet as he watched, the shadow seemed to take on a life of its own, shifting and coiling, forming shapes that danced and flickered in the moonlight.

Cedric felt his pulse quicken as he realized that this was not just any dark magic—it was a concentrated force, a living essence driven by an intent he couldn't yet comprehend.

"Cedric!" Ariana's voice cut through his concentration as she hurried toward him, her face pale but resolute.

"It's getting stronger," she said breathlessly, her eyes scanning the darkness that hovered just beyond the barrier. "It's as if… it's trying to find a way in."

Cedric nodded, his expression grim. "We have to strengthen the wards, but I'm not sure how long they'll hold. This darkness is… it's unlike anything we've faced."

Ariana's gaze hardened, a determined glint in her eyes. "Then we face it head-on. If it wants to test us, let it. We'll show it we're not afraid."

Together, they began chanting, their voices weaving an intricate spell that pulsed with light, reinforcing the barrier with each word. The air vibrated with energy, their combined magic filling the space around them. For a moment, the shadow retreated, shrinking back from the force of their magic.

But just as they thought they had gained the upper hand, the darkness shifted, coiling into itself before forming a figure—a cloaked man, his face obscured but his presence palpable, standing just beyond the reach of their magic.

"Cedric… Ariana…" The figure's voice was low, reverberating through the air like a distant echo. "You cannot hide from me. I have been watching, waiting. You possess power, yes, but it is no match for what lies beyond your understanding."

Cedric felt a chill run down his spine. The figure's voice was familiar, yet distorted, as if layered with the voices of countless others. He took a step forward, his eyes narrowing. "Who are you? What do you want?"

The figure laughed softly, a sound that sent shivers through the night. "I am what you fear. I am the darkness that has always lurked in the corners of your mind. And I am here to remind you that power is not without consequence."

Ariana's hand tightened around her staff, her face set in defiance. "We're not afraid of you," she said, her voice steady. "Whatever you are, you won't find what you're looking for here."

The figure tilted his head, as if amused. "Oh, but I already have." He raised a hand, and the shadows around him seemed to pulse in response. "You see, darkness does not simply take—it gives. And those who embrace it find themselves gifted with power beyond measure."

Cedric felt the air grow heavy, thick with a sense of dread. He could see it now—the figure's intent was not simply to breach their barriers, but to corrupt, to plant seeds of doubt and fear that would undermine their resolve from within.

"Enough," Cedric said, his voice steady but laced with resolve. "You won't find any allies here."

The figure paused, his form flickering like a flame caught in the wind. "Brave words," he murmured, his tone almost admiring. "But bravery alone will not protect you. You may have bound this village with your magic, but darkness is patient. And sooner or later, it will find a way in."

With that, the figure dissipated, the shadows melting into the night. The silence that followed was thick, tense, and filled with an unspoken fear.

Back in their cottage, Cedric and Ariana sat by the fire, the encounter replaying in their minds. The figure's words lingered, a haunting reminder of the danger they faced. Cedric could feel the doubt creeping in, the shadow's influence subtle yet insidious, like a whisper in the back of his mind.

"Do you think he was telling the truth?" Ariana asked, her voice barely above a whisper. "That darkness can... wait us out?"

Cedric shook his head, more to shake off the doubt than to answer her question. "I don't know. But I do know that if we let fear consume us, we're only doing his work for him. We have to stay strong—for each other, and for the village."

Ariana nodded, but her gaze was distant, lost in thought. "Cedric... what if he's right? What if there's a part of us that... that could be swayed?"

He took her hand, his grip firm. "Then we fight it. Just like we fight anything that threatens us. Together."

The days that followed were filled with a quiet vigilance, a tense awareness that hung over the village like a shadow. Cedric and Ariana continued to strengthen the wards, but they could feel the darkness pressing against their defenses, testing them, waiting for a crack to appear.

One night, as Cedric lay in bed, he felt a sudden weight on his chest, as if something were pressing down on him, squeezing the air from his lungs. He opened his eyes to find the room bathed in darkness, thicker than any shadow, as though the night itself had come alive.

"Cedric..." a voice whispered, soft and insidious, echoing the figure's words from the night before. "You cannot hide from me."

He struggled to breathe, to move, but it was as if the darkness had bound him, holding him in place. Panic rose within him, and he felt the edges of his mind fraying, the fear creeping in, urging him to surrender.

But then he felt a warmth beside him—Ariana's hand, resting on his arm, grounding him in the present. Her touch was a lifeline, a reminder of who he was and what he was fighting for. With a surge of determination, he summoned his strength, focusing on the light within him, the light he and Ariana had cultivated together.

The darkness wavered, as if recoiling from his resolve. Slowly, he felt the weight lift, the shadows retreating until he could breathe freely again. He sat up, gasping for air, his heart pounding, but the fear had dissipated, replaced by a fierce determination.

Ariana stirred beside him, her eyes opening to meet his. She didn't need to ask what had happened—she could see the resolve in his gaze, the strength that had been tested and had not broken.

"We're stronger than this," Cedric said, his voice filled with conviction. "Whatever darkness is out there, whatever it wants, it can't take what we've built."

Ariana nodded, a fire kindling in her eyes. "We'll face it, Cedric. Together. And we won't let it win."

As dawn broke over the village, casting a warm light over the sleeping cottages, Cedric and Ariana stood side by side, their hearts and minds as one. They knew the darkness would return, that it would continue to test their resolve, but they were ready.

They had each other, they had the village, and they had the strength of their bond—a light that no shadow could extinguish. And as long as they stood together, they knew that no darkness, no matter how insidious, could ever truly break them.

Chapter 11: The Storm Within

The days following the shadowy figure's appearance brought an eerie calm to the village. Cedric and Ariana felt the tension mounting, a sense that they were standing in the eye of a storm. The villagers, unaware of the malevolent force pressing against their defenses, continued their routines, but Cedric and Ariana noticed a shift—an underlying restlessness, a subtle change in their mood.

The villagers' laughter had softened, their voices quieter, as if the looming darkness had seeped into their spirits without them even knowing. Children played in shorter bursts, their usual carefree energy tempered by a vague unease, and even the village elders, usually a source of calm, seemed troubled.

Despite this quiet unease, Cedric and Ariana remained vigilant, spending countless hours by the village's borders, strengthening the wards and casting protection spells with increasing complexity. But the darkness had its own way of fighting back.

One afternoon, as Cedric was setting new talismans at the edge of the woods, he sensed a chill creeping up his spine. He turned and caught a glimpse of a shadow flitting between the trees. He knew that any ordinary shadow couldn't resist the protective boundary, and yet this one seemed to flicker in and out of view, as if taunting him.

"Show yourself," he commanded, his voice steely, daring whatever presence lurked to come forward.

The shadow hesitated, then coalesced into the familiar figure from the previous night, cloaked and faceless, but with an aura more intense than before. The air felt thick with tension as Cedric gripped his staff, his heart racing.

"I see you're still trying to hold back the inevitable," the figure intoned, its voice a dark whisper that seemed to slip into Cedric's mind like oil on water. "But you're only delaying what's to come. The village cannot stand against the darkness forever."

Cedric felt a surge of anger at the figure's calm arrogance. "You underestimate the strength of this village. We're united, and we're prepared to protect our own."

The figure laughed softly, a sound that grated against Cedric's nerves. "Ah, but unity is a fragile thing, is it not? It only takes a seed of doubt, a whisper of distrust, for the bonds to unravel."

Cedric clenched his fists, refusing to let the figure's words take root. "Whatever you're trying to do, it won't work. We're stronger than you think."

The figure tilted its head, as if amused by Cedric's defiance. "Strength is meaningless if it isn't tested. And I will test you, Cedric, in ways you cannot imagine."

The figure dissolved into the air, leaving behind an unnatural chill that lingered long after it had vanished. Cedric stood there, feeling a weight settle in his chest, a pressure that hadn't been there before. He knew that the darkness was playing with him, trying to sow seeds of doubt, and he couldn't let it succeed.

That night, as Cedric and Ariana gathered with a few of the villagers to perform a ritual of protection, he felt the weight of the figure's words pressing on him. The ritual required each villager to hold a talisman and offer their intention for the village's safety. They moved in a circle, hands linked, and chanted in unison, their voices rising and falling with a rhythm that pulsed through the earth.

But as they reached the climax of the ritual, a strange sensation swept through the circle. Cedric felt it first—a faint pressure in his chest, like a knot tightening around his heart. He could see Ariana's face contort with effort as she fought to keep the ritual's energy steady, but the others looked uneasy, shifting and casting wary glances at each other.

Just as the ritual was about to end, one of the villagers, Mara, suddenly gasped, dropping her talisman as if it had burned her. She stumbled back, her face pale, her eyes wide with terror.

"It's… it's inside me," she whispered, her voice shaking. "I… I can feel it."

The villagers stepped back, murmuring anxiously as Mara's breathing grew erratic. Cedric and Ariana moved toward her, reaching out to calm her, but she recoiled, her eyes darting between them with a wild, fearful look.

"Stay back!" she cried, clutching her arms. "It's your magic—it's what brought this darkness here. You've… you've cursed us all!"

A cold silence fell over the group, the words hanging in the air like a physical weight. Cedric's stomach twisted at Mara's accusation. He could see the confusion in her eyes, the fear that clouded her judgment, but he also knew that this was exactly what the darkness wanted.

"Please, Mara," Ariana said, her voice gentle but firm. "This isn't us. We're here to protect the village. The darkness is trying to turn us against each other."

Mara shook her head, backing away. "But it wasn't here before… before you started all these spells and wards. Maybe… maybe it's drawn to you."

Cedric felt a pang of anger mixed with despair, but he took a deep breath, steadying himself. He understood that Mara's words were driven by fear, not reason, but he also knew that fear could be a powerful tool in the hands of the darkness.

"Listen to me," he said, his voice calm but resolute. "I know you're scared. We all are. But turning on each other will only make it stronger. We have to trust in each other if we're going to survive this."

Mara looked at him, her expression wavering, torn between fear and the desire to believe. After a tense moment, she lowered her gaze, nodding reluctantly. But Cedric could see the seeds of doubt had already taken root.

As the villagers dispersed, Ariana placed a hand on Cedric's shoulder, her eyes filled with worry. "It's happening, Cedric. The darkness is doing exactly what it said it would—turning us against each other."

He sighed, the weight of the situation settling heavily on him. "We need to find a way to counter this, Ariana. If it succeeds in spreading fear, it won't need to breach our barriers—the village will tear itself apart from within."

They spent the rest of the night in deep discussion, going over every spell and ward they had cast, trying to pinpoint any possible vulnerability. But the darkness was clever, slipping through cracks they couldn't see, exploiting the villagers' fears with an ease that was both chilling and infuriating.

Over the next few days, the tension in the village grew. Cedric and Ariana could feel the undercurrent of unease spreading like a silent infection. Villagers whispered in corners, casting suspicious glances at each other, and every small mishap or strange occurrence seemed to fan the flames of their fear.

The final blow came one evening when a fire broke out in the blacksmith's workshop. The flames rose quickly, crackling and consuming everything in their path. Cedric and Ariana rushed to help, casting spells to contain the blaze, but the damage was done. The blacksmith, a burly man named Roderic, turned to them with a look of accusation in his eyes.

"This… this isn't natural," he growled, his face contorted with anger. "None of this was happening before you started your magic. Maybe Mara was right. Maybe you're the reason this darkness is here."

The murmurs of agreement rippled through the crowd, and Cedric felt a pang of frustration. He had spent years protecting this village, dedicating himself to its safety, and now they were looking at him as though he were the enemy.

Ariana stepped forward, her voice strong and unwavering. "This darkness isn't here because of us—it's here because it feeds on fear and doubt. And right now, you're giving it exactly what it wants."

Her words cut through the crowd, silencing them, but Cedric could see that the doubt still lingered, an insidious shadow lurking behind their eyes. He knew that the darkness had gained a foothold, and it would take more than words to root it out.

That night, as they sat by the fire, Cedric looked at Ariana, his face etched with exhaustion. "How do we fight something that can't be seen, that can slip into people's hearts and minds without them even realizing it?"

Ariana took his hand, her gaze steady. "We stay strong, Cedric. We don't let it turn us against each other. And we keep reminding them of what's real—the bonds we've built, the trust we share. It's the only way."

They stayed up late, drawing strength from each other, their resolve hardening. They knew the road ahead would be fraught with challenges, that the darkness would not relent. But they also knew that as long as they stood together, as long as they refused to let fear rule them, they had a fighting chance.

And as the first light of dawn broke over the village, Cedric felt a renewed sense of purpose. The darkness might be powerful, but so was the light they carried within. And for as long as he and Ariana stood side by side, he believed they could withstand any storm—even the one that loomed just beyond the horizon.

Chapter 12: The Heart of Darkness

The dawn brought a brief reprieve, but Cedric and Ariana knew it was fleeting. They felt the village's pulse—unsteady, vulnerable, and still tinged with doubt. The dark force outside their borders was weaving itself into the fabric of their lives, and if they didn't act swiftly, it would unravel everything they'd built.

Cedric had spent the early morning hours preparing for a journey. He realized that confronting this force required more than warding spells and rituals; it demanded knowledge. Ancient knowledge. He knew of a forgotten library tucked away in the mountains, a place whispered about in the lore of old spellcasters. Legends said it held records of entities that had plagued villages for centuries, records that could offer insights into weaknesses and ways to banish them. It was a dangerous journey, but he knew it was their best chance.

When he told Ariana, she looked at him with both admiration and concern. "You're taking a great risk, Cedric," she said, her eyes searching his. "What if this darkness moves while you're gone?"

"That's why I need you here, Ariana," he replied, taking her hands. "You're just as powerful as I am, and the village trusts you. You can keep them safe. This is something I need to do alone."

Ariana's grip tightened, reluctance etched on her face. She nodded, understanding yet fearing the unknown dangers he would face. "Promise you'll return," she whispered, her voice barely audible.

"I promise," he said, hoping his own words would make it true.

With that, he packed his things, leaving behind a part of himself with Ariana and the village. He set out just before the sun fully rose, the shadows of the forest casting long, ominous shapes on the path ahead.

The journey was grueling, and Cedric felt the weight of the village's fate pressing on his shoulders with every step. The dark figure's words still echoed in his mind, an insidious whisper threatening to undermine his resolve. As he reached the foothills of the mountains, the air grew thin, and the landscape became increasingly barren, as if life itself had shrunk away from this place.

After hours of climbing, he found himself standing before a narrow crevice between two towering cliffs. He'd heard that this hidden entrance led to the library, but standing before it, he felt a chill that went deeper than the mountain air. He entered, squeezing through the passage, his fingers brushing against the cold stone as he descended into the darkness below.

The library was as silent as a tomb. Stone shelves stretched endlessly in every direction, stacked with scrolls and ancient texts that crackled with age. The faint smell of dust and ink hung in the air, remnants of knowledge from another era. Cedric lit a small spell to illuminate his way, casting a soft, bluish glow around him.

Hours turned into days as he combed through the records, searching for anything that could help him understand the darkness encircling his village. Many of the texts were written in languages he barely recognized, and the ones he could read described battles with forces that seemed insurmountable. Yet, there was a pattern—an understanding that some creatures fed on more than just fear; they thrived on divisions, on eroding the unity of those they sought to destroy.

Finally, as his energy waned, Cedric found what he had been searching for: an old parchment detailing a ritual to summon the true form of a shadow entity, forcing it into a weakened state. It required a deep, unbreakable bond between those performing it—a bond forged in trust and love, for only that could counter the insidious grip of fear the entity thrived upon.

A wave of realization washed over him. This battle wasn't just about magic and spells; it was about holding the village together with the only force that could banish darkness: unity. It was a test of willpower, a challenge to see if they could rise above their own doubts and fears.

Cedric gathered the parchment, tucking it carefully into his satchel. His mind was already racing, formulating a plan as he made his way back to the village. It would take immense effort, but he believed that if he and Ariana could lead the ritual with the villagers by their side, they could turn the tide.

Days later, Cedric arrived back at the village, weary but resolute. The villagers greeted him with a mix of relief and wariness, a reminder of the doubts that still lingered. But Ariana's face lit up with hope as she saw him return, and he felt his own strength renewed.

He gathered the villagers that evening, and together with Ariana, he explained the ritual and what it would require of each of them. "This darkness feeds on our division," he said, his voice steady but passionate. "It preys on our doubts, our fears, and it uses them against us. If we're to banish it, we have to stand together, as one. We must trust each other completely."

The villagers exchanged uncertain glances, some visibly skeptical. But Ariana stepped forward, her voice calm and reassuring. "Cedric has always been here for us, protecting us without hesitation. If we want to save our village, we need to believe in each other, just as he believes in us."

Her words touched something in them, and one by one, the villagers agreed, their fears melting into a shared determination. They gathered around the village center, forming a wide circle, with Cedric and Ariana standing in the middle.

The ritual began as they joined hands, each person silently committing to the unity they would need to drive out the darkness. Cedric and Ariana chanted the ancient incantation, their voices harmonizing as they invoked the force of trust and love that bound them all.

As the incantation reached its peak, a low, rumbling sound filled the air. The shadowy figure emerged at the edge of the village, drawn forth by the strength of the ritual. But this time, it didn't linger in the background—it was pulled toward them, as if against its will. The entity writhed, trying to escape, but the unity of the villagers held it in place.

Cedric felt the strain of the magic as he focused on keeping the connection strong. The entity twisted and shifted, revealing glimpses of its true form—a creature of pure darkness, with eyes that glowed a sickly, unnatural hue. It was furious, lashing out with waves of fear that swept through the circle, but the villagers held their ground, refusing to let it penetrate their unity.

In a final act of defiance, the creature let out an ear-splitting shriek, attempting to sow panic among them. But Ariana's voice cut through the chaos, clear and unwavering: "We are stronger than your darkness. You hold no power here."

With a final, desperate surge, the entity dissolved into wisps of shadow, its power crumbling under the weight of the village's unity. Silence fell over the village as the last remnants of darkness faded, leaving only the steady glow of their joined hands.

Cedric and Ariana looked at each other, their faces filled with relief and gratitude. They had faced the darkness not just with magic, but with the strength of a community that had found its way back to trust. The villagers embraced, feeling a profound sense of connection, a bond forged in the crucible of fear and overcome by their collective will.

In the days that followed, life returned to normal. Laughter and warmth returned to the village, the shadows replaced by a renewed sense of camaraderie. The trials they had faced left an indelible mark, but it was a reminder of what they could achieve together.

Cedric and Ariana knew that challenges would come again, but they felt prepared. They had seen the strength that lay within their village—a strength that went beyond spells and wards, rooted in unity and the resolve to protect each other.

And as they walked through the village hand in hand, they carried a newfound certainty that whatever darkness they might face in the future, they would always have the light within them to guide the way.

Chapter 13: The Dawn of a New Era

As the village settled back into a rhythm of peace, Cedric and Ariana felt a quiet satisfaction in the air, like the calm after a storm. The darkness had tested them all, but now a sense of renewal replaced the tension that once defined each day. People who had been skeptical of one another now exchanged warm greetings, their conversations less guarded, their laughter louder. It was as if the village itself had exhaled, releasing a breath held tight through countless nights of fear.

One morning, Cedric gathered the village elders and a few of the villagers who had shown courage during the ritual. He wanted to discuss not only what they had overcome but how they could prepare for any future threats, without waiting until the last moment. "We've been through a dark trial," he began, his voice calm yet serious. "But I believe it's a chance for us to build something lasting, something that will protect us for generations."

The villagers listened intently as he outlined his vision: creating a council of protectors who would safeguard the village, trained in both practical defense and the ancient arts that could shield against magical threats. He emphasized that this wasn't just about spells and power; it was about maintaining the unity they'd found in their darkest hour.

A woman named Mira, known for her quiet strength and wisdom, raised her hand. "Cedric, many of us have little knowledge of magic. Can ordinary people like us truly defend against something as powerful as what we faced?"

Cedric nodded thoughtfully. "I believe that strength doesn't just come from magic but from resilience and courage. Each of us has something to contribute, whether it's knowledge of the land, the ability to heal, or even the wisdom to guide others. What we faced was formidable, but it thrived because we were divided. Now, we know how powerful we are when we stand together."

Ariana added, "We'll provide training, support, and guidance, so everyone has the chance to strengthen their skills, magical or not. We don't have to wait for darkness to arrive at our doorstep to be prepared."

The idea resonated with the villagers, who had witnessed firsthand the strength of unity. They agreed to form the council and committed to regular gatherings to share knowledge and hone their abilities. Elders would teach the younger generations, who would in turn share new insights, ensuring that the village's defenses were both traditional and forward-thinking.

As the council took shape over the following months, Cedric and Ariana marveled at the transformation in their community. People who once saw each other as mere neighbors were now close friends and allies. New leaders emerged, individuals who had found courage in themselves that they never knew existed. Mira, for example, became one of the council's most respected members, sharing her understanding of the village's plants and herbs for both healing and protection. Her knowledge became invaluable, reminding everyone that strength came in many forms.

Cedric also noticed how Ariana had grown. Her leadership had blossomed, and her confidence was evident in the way she guided others through spellwork and practical lessons. Together, they became the foundation of a new era, a shift that everyone could feel. They were not just protectors— they were teachers, partners, and friends to the people they had once simply defended from afar.

One evening, as Cedric and Ariana watched the council practice under the glow of the setting sun, Cedric felt a wave of pride and contentment. The village was safe, but more than that, it was prepared. They had a community that could face challenges not just with fear, but with courage and unity.

"This is what I always dreamed of," he said softly, turning to Ariana. "Not just safety but true strength, built from within."

Ariana smiled, linking her arm with his. "We built this together, Cedric. The darkness tried to pull us apart, but it only brought us closer. It showed us what really matters."

As they stood together, they both felt that this was just the beginning. The village had a renewed purpose, and with it came a quiet strength that would outlast any shadow. They had all learned that while darkness might visit them again, it would never hold the same power. The people of the village now understood that true light came from within, from the bond they shared and the love that connected them all.

The dawn of a new era had begun. And with it, Cedric and Ariana felt ready to face whatever lay ahead, together.

Chapter 14: Reunion and Resolve

The air was thick with smoke and shouts as Cedric stumbled through the remnants of battle, searching desperately for Ariana. The lush valley of Aeris, once a place of peace and refuge, now bore the scars of war. Fires burned in pockets across the landscape, and the sky above churned with unnatural clouds summoned by the rage of King Thaddeus Aether's dark magic.

Cedric's heart hammered as he scanned the chaos around him, his mind racing with images of Ariana's last moments beside him before they were separated in the skirmish. His connection to her had never felt so intense, but the battle's thickened energies clouded his senses, making it difficult to find her. Fear clawed at him, but he pushed it aside, focusing on the faint sense of her presence he could still feel—like a thread pulling him forward.

"Cedric!" A familiar voice called from behind. It was Eamon Gale, the rogue with a heart as fierce as the winds themselves.

"I can't find her, Eamon," Cedric said, his voice thick with worry.

Eamon put a steadying hand on his shoulder. "She's out there. I know she wouldn't let herself be taken down easily. Remember, she's as stubborn as you are."

They shared a grim smile, both holding onto the sliver of hope that Ariana was fighting just as hard somewhere nearby. "We have to keep moving," Cedric said, nodding with renewed determination. "We'll find her."

Meanwhile, not far from the main battlefield, Ariana leaned against a rock, her breath coming in labored gasps. Her golden hair was streaked with ash, her skin scraped and bruised, yet her sky-blue eyes blazed with an unyielding fire. She clutched her side, where a cut bled through her torn tunic, but the pain only fueled her resolve. She had seen Cedric across the battlefield earlier, their eyes meeting in a brief, fierce moment before the king's soldiers surged between them, pushing them apart.

But she would find him again, she was certain. The love they shared was a bond forged through trials, something no king could break.

"Maelis told me you'd be a force to reckon with," a calm voice called from nearby. Ariana turned, and relief flooded her as she saw Maelis Windwhisper, the wise mage who had taught her and Cedric so much.

"Maelis! Thank the skies you're here," Ariana said, relief softening her voice.

The older woman's gaze was both kind and resolute. "Come. I have a way to bring you back to Cedric, but we must hurry. The king's forces grow stronger by the minute."

Ariana nodded, following Maelis as they weaved through the chaos. Each step they took renewed her sense of purpose. She wouldn't let the king destroy Aeris, nor would she let him rob her of the future she and Cedric had fought so hard to protect.

Back on the other side of the valley, Cedric and Eamon crept through the shadows, dodging soldiers and looking for any sign of Ariana. Then, just as despair began to creep in, Cedric felt a shift in the air—a warm current that brushed against his face, gentle yet powerful.

"Ariana," he whispered, his heart leaping.

The wind seemed to carry a faint whisper, her voice somehow reaching him across the distance: "Cedric, I'm coming."

A surge of strength filled him. He turned to Eamon, his voice alive with hope. "She's close. I can feel her."

Before Eamon could respond, a figure appeared in the distance. Her hair, golden even through the haze, streamed like a beacon, guiding him toward her. Cedric broke into a sprint, his heart pounding as he ran to her. Ariana's eyes widened when she saw him, and they collided in a fierce embrace, both clinging to each other with relief and love that words could not capture.

"I thought I'd lost you," he murmured, pressing his forehead against hers.

"Never," she replied, her voice fierce and filled with resolve. "I'd fight through any storm to find you."

They held each other, the world around them fading for a brief, precious moment. Then, as reality settled back in, they knew what they had to do. Their love had reunited them, but their mission wasn't over. King Thaddeus was still out there, and the kingdom's future was still in peril.

Gathering their allies—Eamon, Maelis, and others who had fought beside them—they took refuge in a hidden grove just beyond the main battle lines. Maelis drew a map in the dirt, detailing the path to the king's encampment.

"The king has taken position at the center of his forces, where he believes himself untouchable," Maelis explained. "If we can reach him, there's a chance we can end this—perhaps even make him see the folly of his ways."

Ariana's eyes gleamed with determination. "He's caused enough suffering. We end this here and now, for Aeris, for Aetheria."

Cedric took her hand, his own expression mirroring her conviction. "Together, we're stronger. He won't stand a chance against us."

Their allies prepared with solemn expressions, each of them aware that this would be the final stand. It wasn't just a fight for freedom but a battle for the right to live without fear, to love openly, and to create a kingdom where magic and unity thrived.

As the night descended, they made their move. Under the cover of darkness, they approached the king's encampment. Cedric and Ariana, their air magic in perfect harmony, moved like shadows, carrying their allies on a steady breeze that kept their approach silent. When they reached the heart of the camp, they found the king surrounded by his personal guards, his cold eyes gleaming with a sinister satisfaction.

"Ah, the star-crossed lovers," he sneered as he saw them, though surprise flickered across his face.

Ariana stepped forward, her voice steady and powerful. "Your hatred has poisoned this land for too long. It's time for you to face the consequences of your actions."

King Thaddeus laughed, a cold and mocking sound. "You think your love can defeat me? You're nothing but children dabbling in forces you barely understand."

But as he spoke, Cedric and Ariana linked hands, their magic intertwining. The air around them began to glow, the wind rising into a storm that filled the entire encampment with an electric hum. Their love was their strength, a force that defied the king's hatred and darkness.

For a brief, intense moment, the air pulsed with a shimmering light, brighter than any flame, as Cedric and Ariana unleashed the full power of their bond. Their combined magic was more than just air—it was a pure force of unity, of resilience, of love so profound that it shook the ground beneath them.

King Thaddeus stumbled, his sneer faltering as he felt the strength of their resolve. "This... this is impossible!"

Cedric's voice was calm, filled with a quiet power. "Love is the oldest magic of all, Your Majesty. You may try to break it, but it will always be stronger than fear."

With a final surge, Cedric and Ariana directed their combined energy at the king, enveloping him in a wind that tore through his defenses, stripping him of the dark power he had gathered. The wind swirled around him, forcing him to confront the emptiness within himself.

As the storm subsided, King Thaddeus was left on his knees, stripped of his malice, his strength drained. Cedric and Ariana lowered their hands, both breathing heavily but standing tall, victorious.

Their allies, seeing the king defeated, erupted in cheers. The battle was won, and as dawn broke over Aeris, a new hope filled the air.

The morning light cast a warm glow over the valley as Cedric and Ariana embraced, surrounded by their friends and allies. They had fought for love, for freedom, and for the right to build a future unshackled by fear.

Together, they had not only saved their kingdom but had ignited a new era of unity.

Chapter 15: A Kingdom Reborn

The valley of Aeris was quiet again, but this time it wasn't the quiet of fear or of war—it was the peaceful hush of dawn breaking over a new beginning. As the first rays of sunlight filtered through the trees, Cedric and Ariana walked hand in hand through the heart of what had once been a battlefield. Now, however, the grass seemed to grow taller, the river to flow clearer, and the air itself to hum with a sense of relief and promise.

After the victory, there was still much to do. While King Thaddeus Aether had been defeated, the scars of his reign remained, not only on the land but on the people's hearts. But for the first time in a generation, hope was tangible, and Cedric and Ariana felt its weight resting in their hands like a fragile, beautiful gift.

They made their way to the gathered crowd of townspeople, warriors, and allies who had come together in unity. The air was alive with a sense of celebration mixed with reverence. This was not a typical victory where one side gloried over another—it was a moment of healing, an acknowledgment of the sacrifices made and the promise to rebuild.

Cedric took a deep breath, his heart swelling as he looked at the faces around him—faces of people who had suffered and endured so much, yet who now looked to him and Ariana with trust and admiration. He glanced at Ariana, whose eyes shone with a mixture of pride and humility. She squeezed his hand, silently encouraging him to speak.

"Today," Cedric began, his voice carrying over the crowd, "we stand not as victors in battle, but as partners in the rebirth of this land. We have been through darkness, through fear, and through loss. But together, we have shown that unity, love, and hope are stronger than any force that seeks to divide us."

The crowd murmured in agreement, and Cedric felt his confidence grow. "The rule of King Thaddeus is over, but that does not mean our journey is. Together, we will rebuild Aeris, Aetheria, and every place touched by his reign. Together, we will restore what was lost and build a kingdom founded not on fear but on trust and respect."

Ariana stepped forward, her gaze steady. "We are not here to lead through power or conquest. Cedric and I stand with you as equals, as friends, and as family. Each of you has a place in this new Aetheria, and each of you has a voice that deserves to be heard."

The crowd erupted into applause, and many reached out, their hands raised in a gesture of support and solidarity. The unity that filled the valley was a promise as powerful as any oath—a commitment to a future they would build together.

The weeks that followed were filled with work, but it was the kind of work that brought people together rather than tearing them apart. Cedric and Ariana worked alongside their friends and allies, establishing councils in each village to ensure that everyone had a say in the rebuilding of their homes. The once-faded lands were slowly transformed as people poured their hearts into restoring their towns, farms, and marketplaces.

Maelis Windwhisper, the wise mage who had guided them through so much, served as an advisor, helping shape a system where wisdom and kindness would guide decision-making rather than force or fear. Eamon Gale, their loyal friend and ally, became a leader in his own right, known for his courage and his deep connection with the people. Together, they created a circle of advisors that encouraged collaboration and respect.

Ariana, with her natural gift for connecting with people, traveled to distant villages, listening to their needs and learning about the unique strengths of each community. Cedric, meanwhile, organized groups to restore the forests and rivers, bringing life back to lands that had been scarred by the king's dark magic.

As they worked, Cedric and Ariana grew closer than ever. They shared moments of laughter amid the work, finding joy in the simplest things: a shared meal with friends, the sight of children playing in newly restored fields, or the quiet of a starlit night spent side by side.

One evening, as they stood on a hill overlooking the valley of Aeris, Cedric turned to Ariana, his expression serious but filled with warmth. "We've been through so much together, Ariana. I can't imagine facing any of this without you."

She smiled, her eyes softening as she looked at him. "Neither can I. We've shared more than just a battle—we've shared our dreams, our fears, and our hopes for a better world."

Cedric took her hand, his voice low and earnest. "Then let's make this official. Will you join me not just as my partner in leadership, but as my partner in life?"

Ariana's smile grew, and she nodded, tears glistening in her eyes. "Yes, Cedric. I've always wanted nothing more than to stand by your side, no matter what comes."

As the sun set over Aetheria, Cedric and Ariana made a promise to each other, a vow as powerful as the bond they had forged through their trials. They knew there would be challenges ahead, but they also knew that together, they could face anything.

The years passed, and the kingdom of Aetheria blossomed under their leadership. People thrived, the land flourished, and magic was no longer feared but embraced as a natural part of life. Festivals were held to celebrate the land and the unity that bound its people, and the story of Cedric and Ariana's journey became a tale told around fires, inspiring generations to come.

Aetheria's new era was not without its challenges, but each one was met with the same spirit of resilience and unity that had won the kingdom its freedom. Cedric and Ariana remained dedicated to their people, always remembering the struggles that had brought them here. They governed not from a throne, but from the heart, leading by example and inspiring others to believe in the power of love, unity, and hope.

And so, the kingdom of Aetheria thrived, a testament to the courage and love of two souls who had dared to believe that a better world was possible. Together, they had not only defeated a tyrant but had also transformed a kingdom, building a legacy that would endure for generations. Cedric and Ariana's story became a beacon of hope, a reminder that even in the darkest of times, love and unity could light the way forward.

Chapter 16: The Power of Love

The kingdom held its breath as the final confrontation drew near. Cedric and Ariana had come a long way from the days of exploring hidden forests and honing their powers in secret. Now, with their allies by their side, they stood on the cusp of a battle that would decide the future of Aetheria.

They had gathered outside the looming castle that once stood as a symbol of fear and oppression, its spires cutting into the sky like jagged reminders of Thaddeus Aether's reign. Now, it was surrounded by a coalition of villagers, warriors from Aeris, and other supporters who had come to stand with Cedric and Ariana against the tyrant who had ruled over them for too long.

Cedric tightened his grip on Ariana's hand. Their fingers intertwined, grounding them both in the moment. His heart pounded, but he was no longer afraid. He looked at Ariana, whose calm gaze met his with unwavering determination.

"We're here because of what we believe in," Cedric said softly. "Because of the love and courage that's brought us this far. I wouldn't want to be anywhere else, with anyone else."

Ariana smiled, a glint of fire in her sky-blue eyes. "Nor I. Whatever happens today, we face it together."

With a nod from Maelis Windwhisper, who stood with the other mages near the front lines, they began the final march toward the throne room where Thaddeus waited. As they moved, the winds picked up, swirling around them in a powerful but gentle embrace, as if the very air itself was lending them strength.

The palace doors creaked open, and they stepped inside, where the dim corridors echoed with the footsteps of their small but determined army. The tension was palpable as they moved through the halls that had once been silent witnesses to Thaddeus's tyranny.

Finally, they reached the throne room, a grand hall with walls adorned with tapestries depicting past rulers. At the far end, sitting atop his throne like a viper ready to strike, was King Thaddeus Aether. His face twisted with rage and disdain, and his eyes glowed with a dark, unnatural fire. The throne room was colder than Cedric had expected, the air thick with the king's dark magic.

"So," Thaddeus sneered, his voice echoing through the chamber, "the rebellious commoner and the traitorous princess have come to claim my throne. Do you really think you can win?"

Cedric took a step forward, meeting the king's gaze without flinching. "We're not here to take a throne, Thaddeus. We're here to free Aetheria from the grip of fear and cruelty. Your reign has caused nothing but suffering. Today, that ends."

Thaddeus rose from his throne, his face contorted with fury. "You think you can best me with pretty words and petty rebellion? I am the king, and my power is absolute!"

He raised his hand, and the shadows in the room began to writhe and twist, forming into dark, fearsome figures that loomed toward Cedric, Ariana, and their allies. But before they could reach them, Ariana lifted her hands, calling forth a surge of wind that blasted through the throne room, scattering the shadows and leaving Thaddeus momentarily stunned.

"You may be powerful," Ariana said, her voice clear and strong, "but you don't understand true strength. It comes not from darkness and fear, but from love and unity."

Thaddeus snarled, summoning more shadows to his side. But this time, Cedric stepped forward, his own magic building as he called upon the wind with a strength he had never felt before. The air crackled around him as he lifted his arms, creating a swirling vortex that encircled the king.

"You've used your power to tear this kingdom apart, but we'll use ours to bring it back together," Cedric declared. His voice was calm, but it held a force that seemed to resonate through the very walls.

The vortex grew stronger, and the winds spun faster, fueled by the love and resolve that Cedric and Ariana shared. They could feel their magic intertwining, becoming one as they combined their power. Together, they unleashed a wave of wind that swept through the throne room, scattering the shadows and forcing Thaddeus to his knees.

But the king was not finished. Summoning his final reserves of dark magic, he rose with a roar, his hands glowing with a sinister light as he prepared to strike. Cedric and Ariana braced themselves, focusing all their strength on deflecting the attack.

In that critical moment, they felt something shift within them—a power that went beyond magic. It was the strength of their love, their unwavering commitment to each other and to the people of Aetheria. As their hands clasped tightly, a brilliant light emanated from them, pure and radiant, casting away the shadows that Thaddeus had summoned.

The king faltered, blinded by the light. Cedric and Ariana took the opportunity, pouring every ounce of their combined strength into one final push. The light grew brighter, filling the room with a warmth that seemed to melt away the darkness itself. The throne room, once a place of fear and cruelty, was transformed into a beacon of hope.

Thaddeus let out a final, agonized scream as the light engulfed him, dissolving the last of his dark magic. When the light faded, the room fell silent. Thaddeus lay motionless, the power of his tyranny broken at last.

A collective sigh of relief swept through the hall as the people realized that the battle was over. Cedric and Ariana stood hand in hand, their faces illuminated by the soft glow of the dawn breaking through the shattered windows. They had done it—together, they had freed Aetheria from the grip of a tyrant.

As they looked out over the crowd of allies and villagers who had come to stand with them, they felt an overwhelming sense of peace. They had faced the darkness, and they had won—not through force alone, but through the power of love and unity.

Maelis Windwhisper stepped forward, a proud smile on his face. "You have done what many thought impossible. You've shown that love and courage are the greatest forces of all."

Cedric and Ariana shared a smile, their hearts full. The battle had been long, but they had triumphed. Together, they had brought Aetheria into a new era, one where hope and love would guide its future.

As they walked out of the throne room, hand in hand, they knew that their journey was far from over. There was still work to be done, but they would face it together, side by side, as partners in life and in leadership. And with each step, they felt the promise of a brighter tomorrow—a kingdom reborn, and a future shaped by love.

Chapter 17: A New Beginning

The victory over King Thaddeus left Aetheria with a chance to begin again, free from the darkness that had overshadowed it for so long. As Cedric and Ariana emerged from the palace, they were greeted by cheers, embraces, and tears of relief from the villagers, warriors, and wind-magic wielders who had fought by their side. Their triumph wasn't just a victory for them but for everyone who had suffered and struggled under Thaddeus's rule.

Ariana turned to Cedric, her hand still intertwined with his. "We did it," she whispered, her voice tinged with awe and gratitude. "Aetheria is free."

Cedric smiled, brushing a stray lock of hair from her face. "And now, we get to build the future we've always dreamed of. Together."

Over the next few weeks, Cedric and Ariana worked tirelessly with Maelis, Loriel, Eamon, Ravenna, and Seraphina to restore peace and unity throughout Aetheria. News of Thaddeus's defeat spread rapidly, and with it, a sense of hope returned to the land. Villages once fearful of using magic cautiously began to embrace it, while those who had hidden their powers for years could finally reveal them without fear of persecution.

Ariana's first decree as princess was to lift the longstanding restrictions on magic, allowing those with gifts to practice openly. For too long, magic had been viewed as dangerous and untrustworthy, thanks to Thaddeus's fear of anything that challenged his authority. Now, under Ariana's leadership, magic would be seen as a gift—a means of healing, creating, and uniting.

But even as they celebrated the beginning of a new era, Cedric and Ariana knew that they had work to do in rebuilding the kingdom's trust. There were people who remained wary of magic, who had been taught to fear it for years. Cedric understood this hesitation; after all, he had once feared his own abilities before learning to embrace them.

So, in an effort to bridge this divide, they organized gatherings throughout Aetheria, inviting villagers and townsfolk to watch demonstrations of magic's peaceful and beneficial uses. Healers showed how they could mend wounds with a gentle touch, while wind-magic users like Cedric and Ariana demonstrated how their powers could be used to aid in farming, building, and travel. Slowly, the fear of magic began to dissipate, replaced by curiosity and even admiration.

One sunny morning, Cedric and Ariana stood on the peaks overlooking Aeris, their sanctuary nestled safely within the valley below. The residents of Aeris had offered their support to help lead this new era, promising to provide guidance and training to those eager to explore their abilities. Loriel and Ravenna organized classes for young wind-magic users, helping them learn to control their gifts responsibly and with respect for the natural world around them.

Seraphina Breezewhisper, with her gentle manner and vast knowledge, took on the role of healer for the kingdom, providing aid to those in need and passing down her skills to others willing to learn. She created a space within Aeris where people could come from all over Aetheria to seek help, fostering a sense of community and mutual support.

As they watched the bustling activity below, Ariana turned to Cedric. "It feels like a dream, doesn't it? Seeing people gather here, no longer hiding who they are."

Cedric nodded, a smile playing on his lips. "It does. But it's more than a dream now. It's real. And it's because of what we've accomplished together."

They shared a quiet moment, letting the breeze carry away their words. Cedric felt a deep sense of peace, knowing that the kingdom was finally on a path toward harmony and unity.

A few weeks later, a celebration was held in Aeris to honor the end of Thaddeus's reign and the beginning of a new chapter for Aetheria. Friends, family, and allies gathered in the valley, filling the air with laughter, music, and the sounds of celebration. Lanterns floated into the sky as the sun dipped below the mountains, casting a warm glow over the gathering.

It was during this celebration that Cedric took Ariana's hand and led her to a quiet spot overlooking the valley. The music and laughter faded into the background as he looked into her eyes, emerald meeting sky blue.

"Ariana," he began, his voice soft but steady, "you've been my guide, my friend, my strength. You taught me how to believe in myself, even when I doubted. And every day, you remind me of what it means to love with all my heart. I can't imagine my life without you."

Ariana's eyes shone with emotion as she squeezed his hand. "Cedric, from the moment we met, I knew there was something special between us. You've shown me that love can be a source of strength, a power greater than any magic. I'm so grateful for every moment we've shared, and I want to face whatever lies ahead with you by my side."

In that moment, with the stars beginning to appear overhead, Cedric knelt before her, his heart racing. "Ariana, will you marry me?"

Ariana's face lit up with a radiant smile as she nodded, tears of joy sparkling in her eyes. "Yes, Cedric. A thousand times, yes."

Cheers erupted from the crowd as their friends realized what had happened, and soon they were surrounded by well-wishers, each eager to offer their blessings to the happy couple. Maelis Windwhisper, his eyes twinkling with pride, led a blessing for them, calling upon the wind to protect and guide their love.

A month later, Cedric and Ariana were wed in a beautiful ceremony high above the peaks of Aeris, surrounded by their closest friends and family. The winds carried their vows to each corner of the valley, as if to mark the unity they had forged not just between themselves, but within the kingdom as well.

They stood side by side, looking out over the land they had fought so hard to protect. Together, they had brought peace to Aetheria, and now they were ready to lead it into a future filled with hope and promise.

As they took their first steps as husband and wife, hand in hand, they knew that whatever challenges lay ahead, they would face them together—with love, with courage, and with the winds always at their back, carrying them forward into the dawn of a new beginning.

Chapter 18: A Legacy of Love

Years passed, and Cedric and Ariana's dreams blossomed throughout Aetheria, flourishing beyond what they'd ever imagined. The kingdom, once wary of magic, now embraced it as part of everyday life. People from every corner of the land traveled to Aeris to learn, to share, and to celebrate the new unity of Aetheria's magic and people. Cedric and Ariana, now rulers in both title and spirit, fostered a land where magic was cherished rather than feared, where differences were met with curiosity instead of suspicion.

Cedric had grown into his role as both a leader and a teacher. His calm demeanor and gentle wisdom made him beloved among his people, and he often spent his days guiding young wind-magic users, sharing the lessons he'd learned through trial and triumph. With his help, many who once saw their abilities as a burden found pride in their gifts. As he watched new generations soar, their laughter ringing through the sky, he felt a deep sense of fulfillment. He knew that the journey he and Ariana had undertaken was worth every hardship, every sacrifice.

Ariana, too, had come into her own as a leader. Her compassion and strength inspired the people of Aetheria to embrace their own courage and kindness. She encouraged everyone—magic users and non-magic users alike—to share their skills and knowledge, cultivating a community built on mutual respect. Her role as princess evolved into that of a queen, not through the declaration of her title, but through the respect and love of the people she served. Her vision for Aetheria—one of harmony, strength, and freedom—had come to life.

One evening, as the sky painted itself in shades of pink and gold, Cedric and Ariana gathered with their friends and allies in the heart of Aeris. Maelis Windwhisper, now older and slower in his steps but still sharp of mind, had announced he was ready to pass on his mantle as the keeper of ancient knowledge. He entrusted Cedric and Ariana to preserve and expand the wisdom of the wind magic tradition, confident that they would guide the kingdom into a bright future.

"We've come so far," Ariana said, leaning against Cedric's shoulder as they watched their children, along with other young magic users, laughing and playing in the fields of Aeris. The children wove the wind around them in carefree spirals, their innocence and freedom embodying everything Cedric and Ariana had fought for.

Cedric smiled, his heart swelling with pride. "They're the future, Ariana. They'll take what we've built and make it into something even greater."

Their children—three of them, each with a spark of magic in their eyes and the adventurous spirit of their parents—had grown up with tales of their parents' journey. While young, they were wise in the way children are, attuned to the values of courage, kindness, and love. To them, magic wasn't something to hide but a gift to be shared, a language spoken by the wind, the trees, and the sky.

Cedric and Ariana's eldest, a boy with eyes as green as his father's, had already shown an exceptional talent for guiding the wind. Patient and perceptive, he often observed the world with a keen interest, soaking up stories of Aetheria's past and dreaming of what he could do in its future. Their second child, a daughter with Ariana's sky-blue eyes, was gifted with a radiant kindness that touched everyone she met. She saw magic as a way to heal, much like Seraphina Breezewhisper, and spent her days learning the art of healing. Their youngest, still a toddler, was filled with an endless curiosity and a mischievous smile, his laughter echoing through the valley as he chased after birds in playful flights, already reveling in the freedom of the sky.

Together, Cedric and Ariana nurtured their children's gifts, letting them explore their abilities in the fields of Aeris, much as they themselves had done when they were young. They taught them not only how to use magic but also how to respect it, to see it as part of the world around them rather than something to wield for power. In their children's laughter and joy, they saw the promise of a world that was kinder, more open, and unafraid.

In time, Cedric and Ariana's legacy grew beyond the borders of Aetheria. Other kingdoms took notice of Aetheria's prosperity and peace, marveling at how magic had woven itself into daily life, enhancing agriculture, medicine, and the arts. Delegations arrived, curious and eager to learn from Cedric and Ariana's vision of unity. Cedric welcomed them, sharing stories of their journey, the sacrifices and triumphs that had brought Aetheria to this moment. Through their example, neighboring lands began to shift their own attitudes toward magic, seeing it less as a threat and more as a source of wonder.

Years passed, and Aetheria flourished under Cedric and Ariana's rule. As they grew older, their love only deepened, forged in the fires of adversity and strengthened by the shared vision they had brought to life. They took comfort in knowing that their children would carry on their legacy, each in their own unique way, building upon the foundation they had created.

One quiet evening, Cedric and Ariana stood together at the highest peak of Aeris, the place where they had once exchanged their vows. The stars sparkled brightly above them, their light reflected in the eyes of the couple who had given their all for the future of Aetheria.

Cedric took Ariana's hand, his fingers intertwining with hers as they gazed at the kingdom below. "This is only the beginning," he murmured, his voice filled with quiet awe.

Ariana leaned her head on his shoulder, a smile playing on her lips. "Yes, my love. We've created something beautiful, something that will last long after we're gone. Our love, our vision, will live on in Aetheria and in our children."

As they stood there, the wind gently swirling around them, Cedric and Ariana felt a deep sense of peace. They had given everything to this land, and in return, it had gifted them with a love that transcended time, a legacy that would echo through the generations.

And as the wind carried their laughter, their love, and their dreams into the starlit sky, Cedric and Ariana knew that they had found their place in the world—together, forever woven into the fabric of Aetheria's future, their legacy a guiding force for all who would come after.

With that, Cedric and Ariana's story became legend, a tale passed down through the ages. And long after their time, when people would gaze up at the stars or feel the wind brush their face, they would remember the two who had loved so deeply, who had dared so greatly, and who had left a legacy of unity, courage, and love for generations to come.

Epilogue: Soaring Into the Future

Generations came and went, and the story of Cedric and Ariana wove itself into the essence of Aetheria. In every village, town, and city, people spoke of the couple who had united the kingdom, who had shown that magic was a bridge rather than a barrier. Their legacy lived on, not only in stories but in the spirit of Aetheria itself—a land where magic and humanity had found harmony, each enriching the other.

The kingdom's children grew up with tales of Cedric's courage and Ariana's compassion, of their journey through mountains and forests, their battles and triumphs, and the love that had blossomed along the way. These stories were more than mere legends; they were a guide for future generations, a reminder of the strength that came from unity, and the power of love and resilience.

In the years that followed, Aetheria flourished in ways Cedric and Ariana had dreamed of but had never fully seen in their lifetime. The arts thrived, with magic and creativity intertwining to produce beauty that inspired awe throughout the kingdom. Mages and artisans worked side by side, crafting wonders that enriched the lives of all who beheld them. Farms were nurtured by spells that encouraged bountiful harvests, and healers trained in the wisdom of Seraphina Breezewhisper brought health and comfort to villages across the realm. It was a world where magic was no longer feared, but embraced—a part of everyday life.

A school was established in Aeris, the city that had once been a refuge for magic-users and outcasts. It became a center of learning for all Aetherians, both with and without magic. Teachers, inspired by Cedric and Ariana's vision, educated the young in more than just spells or history. They taught the values of acceptance, courage, and kindness, encouraging each student to find their unique gift—whether it was magic, a talent, or a skill—and to use it for the good of all.

On a quiet hillside near Aeris, a statue of Cedric and Ariana was erected—a tribute not to their royalty but to their legacy. Carved in stone, it showed them standing side by side, gazing forward with determination and tenderness, their hands entwined. The people of Aetheria gathered each year at the statue, telling stories and celebrating the Day of Unity, a holiday commemorating the peace Cedric and Ariana had forged. It was a time for families to come together, to laugh and share dreams for the future. Children ran through the fields, flying kites on the breeze, the same wind that had once been Cedric's closest companion.

In time, Cedric and Ariana's children grew and took up their roles as leaders, each one guided by the values their parents had instilled. They were different in their approaches—some more daring, others more contemplative—but each one worked toward the same vision, determined to continue the legacy their parents had begun. As they ruled and guided Aetheria, they were supported by the love and unity that had been built long before them. They knew that they were not alone; they were part of a long, unbroken chain, a legacy that had begun with a boy with green eyes and a girl with sky-blue dreams.

Decades later, in a quiet moment at dusk, Cedric and Ariana's great-granddaughter, a girl named Elara with the same green eyes and a gift for magic, stood by the statue of her ancestors. She closed her eyes, feeling the breeze caress her face, as if whispering secrets from another time. She thought of the stories she'd grown up with—the tales of adventure and love, courage and sacrifice. She felt a stirring within her, a call to take up the mantle of her heritage, to forge her own path in the kingdom they had left behind.

Elara opened her eyes and smiled. She knew that the story of Cedric and Ariana was not over; it would continue to unfold, passed down through each generation, guiding Aetheria into the future. The legacy they had left was more than a kingdom or a title. It was a vision of hope, of courage, and of unity, a reminder that even the most ordinary people could change the world if they dared to believe in the power of love.

As she turned to leave, Elara lifted her hand, letting the wind play through her fingers, just as her great-grandfather once had. And as she walked away from the statue, she could almost hear the laughter of Cedric and Ariana, echoing through the breeze, soaring ever forward into a future they had dreamed of but left for others to build.

In Aetheria, under the boundless sky, the wind carried their legacy onward, whispering to all who would listen—a story of love and magic that would never be forgotten.

About The Author

Julianna Cubbage

Julianna Cubbage is a contemporary author who seamlessly bridges the worlds of romance, science fiction, and horror fiction. Her unique perspective as a former quantum physics researcher at MIT infuses her storytelling with a distinctive blend of scientific precision and emotional depth.

After trading her laboratory coat for a writer's desk in 2018, Cubbage quickly established herself as a voice to watch in multiple genres. Her debut novel, which merged quantum physics concepts with a love story, caught the attention of both romance readers and science fiction enthusiasts, earning her recognition as an innovative cross-genre author.

Known for her meticulous research and character development, Cubbage approaches her craft with the same analytical mindset she once applied to scientific experiments. Her horror works are particularly noted for their psychological complexity and integration of scientific concepts, while her romance novels stand out for their intellectually stimulating plots and unconventional meet-cutes.

Based in Providence, Rhode Island, Cubbage divides her time between writing and teaching creative writing at the local community college. She lives with her two cats, endearingly named after famous physicists, and frequently participates in both literary and scientific conferences, where she discusses the intersection of science and storytelling.

Her work often explores themes of parallel universes, quantum entanglement as a metaphor for relationships, and the terrifying implications of scientific advancement. Critics have praised her ability to make complex scientific concepts accessible while maintaining emotional authenticity in her characters.

Cubbage is currently developing a new series that ambitiously combines all three of her preferred genres into what she describes as "quantum gothic romance," a subgenre she might well be pioneering.